VEGAS
CRUSH

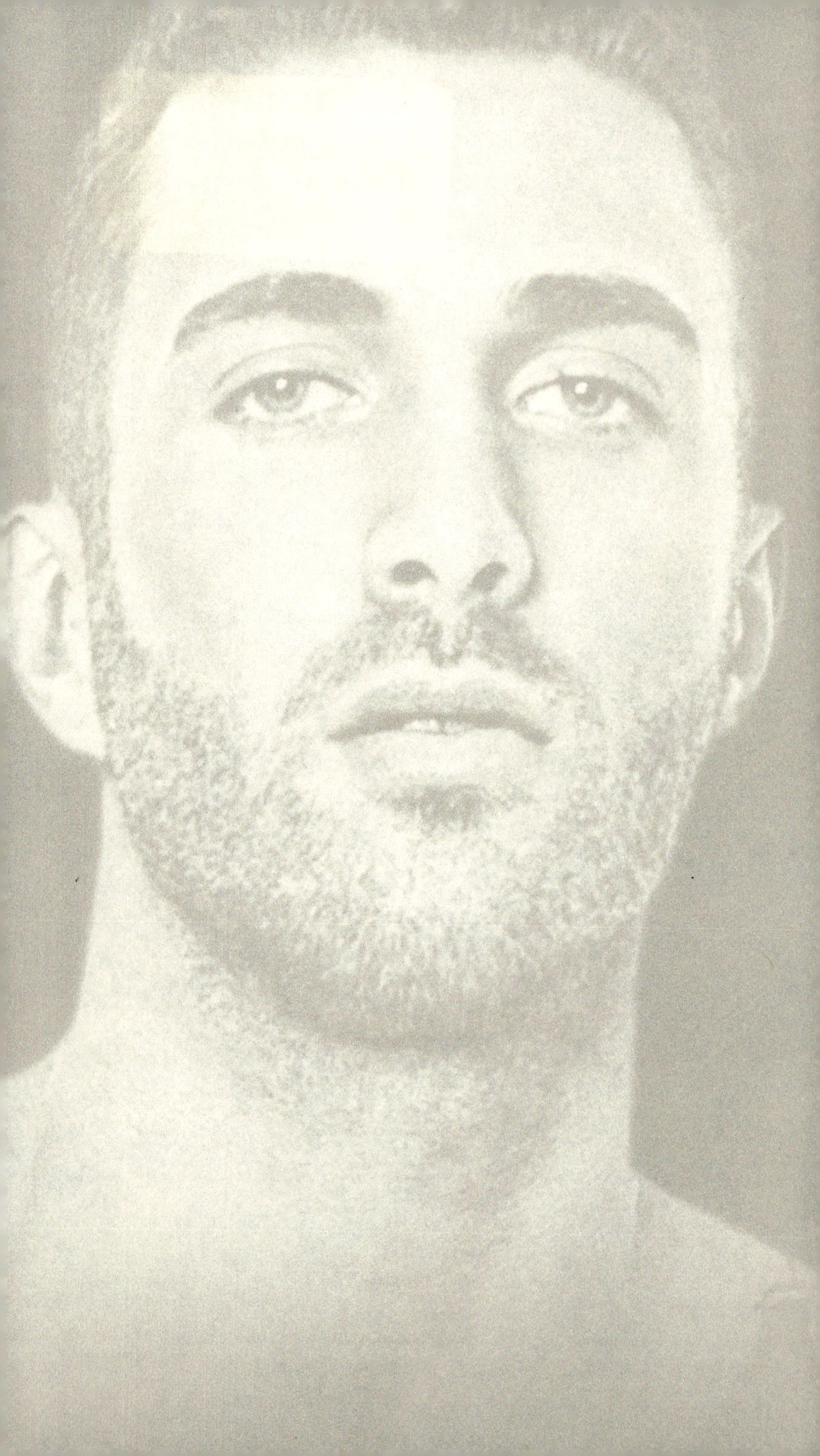

NEW YORK TIMES BESTSELLING AUTHOR
RAINE MILLER
writing as Brit DeMille
PUCK Money
HOME OF THE VEGAS CRUSH
BORIS DRĂGHICI CENTER
VEGAS CRUSH

Raine Miller Romance

# boris drăghici

Center

4

# dedication

*For those who are,*
*and always will be...*
*VEGAS STRONG.*

# 1
# enter the ice dragon

Boris

Saving a terrified mother and her screaming child from disaster in the Las Vegas Airport baggage claim wasn't on my to-do list today. But what else do you do when a woman is fighting to keep her stroller from crashing down the escalator, her child screaming bloody murder as I head down to the baggage claim. Potentially a straight-out disaster in the making, I feel bad for both of them. I steady the stroller when it tilts to the next step as she pulls her crying toddler into her arms. Once we're on solid ground, she gives me an apologetic smile, a soft, "Thanks," and rushes the whole mess into the nearest restroom.

Disoriented, I look around and find the amiable smile of my agent, Scott Rose, where he stands with a few other guys. Everyone holds a sign with a name on it, apart from Scott. I point to the signs. "No 'Welcome Ice Dragon' sign?"

"Sorry, bro." He grins and gives me a friendly slap

on the back. "How was your flight? I see you started do-gooding right off the bat. That's nice what you did for that lady."

"Is do-gooding a real word? My English is pretty strong but that is a new one for me."

"Come on, let's go grab your bags, do-gooder."

Bags in tow, my agent leads me out into the hot Las Vegas sun. We cross four lanes of traffic and head to the short-term parking, where Scott's Mercedes SUV is parked. It's shiny and white and very, very clean. Kind of like Scott, I suppose. He's slick as all get-out in his suit, no tie, and I feel a bit underdressed in jeans and a button-down as I climb in. I will say I'm glad I am not in a suit, though, because I'd be sweating like crazy. Apparently, Scott Rose does not sweat.

"I'll get the air going," Scott says as he starts the engine. "It's hot as dragon's breath out here today."

"Hotter than Austin," I comment. "How is that possible? It must be ten degrees hotter here and Austin is further south."

"One of life's great mysteries, the weather. I think hockey players are somewhat more sensitive to the heat, though, since they're on the ice all the time."

"Perhaps that is true."

"You excited about moving to Sin City?"

I nod. "It is more the team that excites me. I like what I have seen from the lineup."

"A city full of gorgeous women, plentiful liquor, and endless nightlife, and your head is already on the game. I knew there was a reason I took you on. I wish I had ten of you on my client list. Easy peasy."

"I am a boring guy," I say with a shrug.

"Not on the ice, though. There's a reason they call you the Ice Dragon. You're one of a very short list of the NHL's best forwards. Play you with Evan and Mikhail on wings, Georg and Viktor on defense, damn. Can't wait to see what you all can do out there, and I don't care what the rabble-rousers are saying online. Evan and Georg are still among the best on the ice."

"People are saying otherwise about them online?" I press.

"Bah," Scott grunts, waving off the question. "Fall from grace, lucky championship season, aging players. You know, same old garbage, different day. Some even say they've gone soft since settling down. Frankly, I'm glad Georg isn't dead from liver failure. I'll take a sober, serious, and much less reckless Georg any day."

"He was a wild man," I agree. "Hey, thanks for your help with the contract negotiations."

"That's my job, buddy. You ready for the big pressure, though? You're here to make sure those yahoos stay on their top game. To add to the good mojo. Max Terry wants that cup again. Wants to prove it's not just a fluke out here."

"Big pressure comes with big paychecks," I answer, watching the Strip come into view. There are so many people. It's still midday, so I'm sure I'm not getting the full view of the famous area with its lights and fountains. But I get an idea, just from the masses of people, tourists with cameras, taking selfies with their phones, carrying shopping bags.

"Quite the place, huh?" Scott gives me a look. "You've never been out on the Strip before?"

"Not really. I didn't go out exploring the times we came in to play the Crush."

"Well, this city is a distraction. Be careful not to let it shift your focus. Just ask Georg how easy it is."

"Georg could be distracted by a paper bag." I'm not lying. Georg has always been that way. He and I are distant cousins, so I have many memories from when we were kids. Well, his father and my mother are cousins, somehow way back in the bloodlines. It's complicated in the way that families are complicated with marriages and divorces and babies, and the rest of what comes with that. We saw each other at family gatherings, and hockey events too, but a lot more after my mother moved us back to her native Saint Petersburg.

"If there was a liquor bottle in it," Scott says.

"True," I say, nodding. "He's clean this past year though, I heard. Right?"

Scott bobs his head in affirmation. "Clean. Married. Focused. I took him on once I saw how good he could be when he wasn't dicking around."

"I am excited to play with him again. It's been a while since we've been on the ice together, but what I'm really looking forward to is playing with him on the same team."

"He had raw talent then. He's really grown into it

now. It's much more powerful. Very exciting to watch."

"I remember from the playoffs," I say with a nod. "He was a surprise on the ice."

"To us all, buddy," Scott agrees. "To us all."

We pull into a garage system that looks attached to a hotel, dropping the vehicle with a valet who asks for a selfie and tells me how awesome it is that I've come to play here. We walk out into the hot sun, traveling on foot for a block before heading into the arena where I will play very soon.

Inside the owner's suite, Max Terry and I shake hands and then he tells me basically everything Scott just said on the way from the airport. He wants another chance at the cup, and he thinks this is the lineup to make it happen. And I can't deny that he's right. On paper, at least.

He hands me an envelope, which he describes as a "Welcome letter," and I find myself frowning at the inoffensive piece of paper for long enough that I realize it probably sends the wrong message, so I fold it, shove it in my back pocket, and force a smile to make sure no one gets the wrong impression.

Too late, though, as Max asks, "Are you unhappy with this trade, Boris?"

I shake my head rapidly. "No, not at all."

"Your contract was satisfactory, I assume? I mean, you signed it," he says. "I assumed this acquisition was a good one for us and for you. The numbers we put up were quite generous."

"No, I apologize," I say quickly. "Everything is in

order on all fronts. I think I'm just a bit jet-lagged from the early morning flight."

"Ah, good." The handsome, well-dressed, silver-haired owner claps his hands once. "This is a tremendous acquisition for our team. We want to make sure you come in with good feelings. Get off on the right foot."

"Both feet are here in Las Vegas and I feel good," I assure him. "I just want to play hockey, sir."

# 2
# a total rebuild

Talia

I have about fourteen boxes of paperwork to fit into three drawers of a file cabinet. It's actually surprising how much business my boss, Harold Shaw, managed here in Vegas, even from his home base in San Francisco. He sent me here with the historical files, even for clients we no longer manage. Now I have this monumental logistics issue to figure out.

Maybe someday I'll convince him we need another person here, just an administrative assistant to help digitize the files, answer the phones, manage the calendars. Good thing I can do all of that too—otherwise, I'd be tearing my hair out right now.

I mean, I guess it makes sense that a financial advisor would be somewhat organized, right? It would be weird if I was really good at analyzing market performance and investment strategy but unable to figure out how to organize a few files.

When Harold offered me the opportunity to

rebuild Baseline Investments here in Vegas, I jumped on it in a heartbeat. He once had a respectable market share here among the sports and entertainment professionals, but he has many high-profile clients in San Francisco now and he can't get down here as often. Some of his clients have moved to other markets and are handled by other members of the team. He realized this was an untapped market, ready for someone hungry to come in and build it back up.

I mean, I know it was a favor, too. This opportunity spared me the need to dig a hole and jump inside. He's been supportive and discreet, but it's never a good thing when your boss realizes you've been sleeping with a client. A very rich, very married, very important client.

I can't stomach seeing the guy and Harold can't stomach losing me from the team, so this is our compromise.

This office is a box. It's probably ten feet wide by seventeen feet long with one window to the outside world and a tiny, attached bathroom. It's nothing special, and I know it's temporary, only until I can get enough clientele booked to justify a better space, but still. It's kind of a hole. Well, I guess I did jump in a hole after all, now, didn't I?

*A hole you dug for yourself, one shovelful at a time.*

I push my glasses up and gaze out at the street below. It's busy with what I presume is a wide mix of tourists and locals. My office is not quite on the Strip, thankfully, but it's close enough, and there is a row of restaurants just outside my office doors. I found an apartment within a safe walking distance, though I bought pepper spray and a set of knuckledusters that both hang on my key ring just in case.

My first client of the day comes wandering in as I'm staring outside. The sound of the bells on the door make me jump to attention. I smooth my skirt and toss my long hair behind my shoulders as I reach out to shake his hand.

"Imari," I say, "good to see you again."

"Thought I might not see you again after I moved here. Good news for me, you got traded, too."

I grin. Imari is tall and lean, a forward who played for Golden State until he broke his leg. He started coaching for the Dons in San Francisco and came to us for money management advice. Namely, he wasn't making as much as an offensive coach as he'd been making as a pro player, and he needed to figure out how to better protect what he had. Now he's head coach at UNLV and feeling much more comfortable with his salary.

"Sorry for the mess." I look around and realize I don't have a chair to offer him, so I move two boxes to the floor to open up one of the guest chairs before heading around to my office chair to pull out his files.

"Why no assistant? This place is like a little, tiny prison. You get promoted or put in prison, Talia?"

I laugh. Probably too loud because I'm socially awkward like that. And he kind of hit the nail on the head. It's both a chance to build my client list and serve a good strong dose of career-purgatory as punishment for doing something very, very stupid.

"Maybe both?" I answer, cringe-smiling. Ever done that? Smile and cringe at the same time? It mostly looks like you're passing gas. Not pretty. I school my face to what I hope is neutral and add, "Harold wants me to get a few new clients before he'll spring for extra help. A few more than that and I may be able to get new digs. So please go out and say nice things about me to people who need an awesome financial advisor. Baby wants a new office chair."

"I've already done that, girl. Expect a few calls in the next week, for sure."

"Yay. You're the best." I offer a fistbump, which he reciprocates. "Speaking of...how's your better half?"

"Shai's good," he says. "And the girls are growing up fast. They're having their seventh birthday party in a month and they literally won't stop talking about it. You should come if you're into that sort of thing."

Imari has twin girls with his wife, Shai. They are such a nice family; I just adore them. Which is why I spend an awful lot of time analyzing and adjusting his portfolio. He got a bum, random deal when it came to that injury. He was expecting to be able to play for at least ten more years and losing that time meant he had to face some unexpected realities when it came to his long-term financial plans.

"Seven-year-old birthday parties are my jam, so you can count me in. I'm reserving my own personal jumping session in the bouncy castle right now, so tell Shai."

"On it." He laughs at my ridiculousness and taps something into his phone. "Done."

"Well, then, I'll be on the lookout for my invitation. You'll be pleased to hear I have good news that I can't wait to share with you." I veer us back on track to the purpose of this visit.

As we go over his financial statements, I show him a recent change-up I made to his investment portfolio, pointing out various line items of note. "The market is super volatile right now, so I wanted to make sure that the bulk of your money was as bulletproof as possible. So, I moved these assets over here, but then put a chunk that was languishing in mediocre-town and threw it into these hot stocks. I watched and when they went high, I sold and then reinvested in a medium-risk mix. The value was instantly higher and should now have medium growth, with little chance of getting hit hard by market unpredictability."

"Wow, Talia, you're a genius. I didn't know portfolio advisors could be so nimble. What a great strategy."

"Well, I aim to please. And remember, I had you sign off so I could have that level of flexibility in decision-making. Other advisors could do it, but it would mean monitoring accounts individually on a day-to-day basis and most don't want to do that much work."

"What do people pay them for, then?"

I shrug. "The investment process is pretty complicated, and it does take an expert to make discerning choices at the right moment. Most good advisors can get great results without this level of service. I just like to play with the puzzle pieces when

I can, when I'm feeling confident of a sure bet. Maybe there will come a day when I can't do this level of hyper-focus on accounts, but for now, I have the time and interest. Especially for my favorite clients." I give him a playful wink.

He presents his knuckles for a second fistbump as we finish up his review. Once we're done, I walk him to the door. He gives me a side-hug, made awkward by the fact that he's like a foot taller than I am, before heading out into the afternoon sun. And I smile. Looks like I'll have at least two friends in Las Vegas, after all.

I DON'T HAVE other client appointments today, so I hunker down in front of my computer to watch how the markets finish, then make some notes on a few clients' accounts I want to change up. Before I know it, it's past nine and my stomach reminds me I've missed dinner. Again.

After locking up, I make the short walk to my apartment. I was lucky to find something affordable, with a doorman and security system, right within actual walking distance of the office. I like living among the hustle and bustle of the high-traffic area just off the Strip. It makes me feel like I'm part of something and feeling part of something is enough for me, since I'm an introvert by nature.

Inside my small studio apartment, I hear the

tinkle of my cat's little collar bell as she runs toward me, welcoming me home.

"Good evening, Miss LuLu," I say, picking her up. She rubs against my face and purrs before squirming away and running toward the kitchen area. "I'm sorry I'm late. You must be starving."

I get LuLu fed, then heat up another culinary delight from my freezer (chicken enchiladas suizas) and make a cup of tea before settling on my blue velvet chaise with a book. My apartment is exactly two and a half rooms—the studio living space, a bathroom, and a tiny kitchenette space separated from the main living area by a small buffet bar and two stools. I've got a chaise lounge, one of my handmade chenille blankets (hand knit by *moi*), and two full bookcases. It works for me.

I start reading the John le Carré thriller my dad gave me for Christmas in between bites of enchilada, the heavy hardback tome awkard to manage with LuLu and my dinner plate in my lap. But I have some serious experience doing the cat/book juggle—which becomes a lot easier once the dinner is eaten—and settle in to read some more. I keep nodding off, but I don't stop to force myself into my bed or anything sensible like that.

No, I just keep on reading, or attempting to.

Eventually, I fall asleep on the chaise with LuLu and my open book on my chest...with my glasses still on my face.

Again.

At least my life's predictable.

# 3
# something in the water

Boris

"It's so good to see you, *moya kuzina*," Georg says as he spots me on the bench press. "And good to see that your summer of leisure didn't diminish your gym routine."

I laugh at this and shake my head before grabbing the weighted bar and pressing it to my chest, working through ten reps before setting it back on the rack. "I know. I look good. You look as scrawny as ever, though," I joke back.

Georg flexes his bicep and says, "Scrawny? No, lean and fit and sexy, so says my woman."

"I'm sure she loves being called that," I say, still laughing. "American women love being treated as if they are items to be owned, I hear."

"You hear? You mean you haven't had an American woman?"

"I am not a monk, Georg, as you are well aware." *And it's time to change the subject.* "Why is the gym so empty today?"

"Some summer commitments are not yet finished. Russian league just finished. Pam and I got back three days ago but some stay for time with family," Georg says as I pull another set. "Practice starts in one week. They will wait until the last minute to return."

"It was like that in Austin, though many came back a few days early to party."

Georg grins and wiggles his eyebrows. "Partying happens all season long here."

"Not for you anymore, I hear."

"That is true. Why didn't you go back home for summer league?" he asks.

I finish my last set on the bench and sit up. Georg adjusts the weight so he can do his sets. I rib him for switching to a lighter weight and he says he's sure he can lift heavier but why bother when there is no one important around to see it?

Shaking my head, I answer his question about summer. "I had a mild concussion at the end of the season and was advised not to play summer league." I pause momentarily, curious why Georg didn't know about my injury. *Too busy with his American woman is my guess.* "So, I stayed in Austin and ran an ice hockey camp for kids instead."

"You ran a camp?"

"Yes. I really enjoyed it."

"Ick. Kids. Who would want to be around kids all day every day like that?"

"You don't like children?"

"They're okay at a distance, I suppose."

"What about your *woman*? Doesn't she want to have kids?"

"Now who's being sexist?" Georg asks, laughing. "No, not anytime soon. She says I'm barely an adult myself and she doesn't need anyone else to take care of in her life right now."

"Ouch."

"It is the cold truth, my brother. I hope I never knock her up. I'd be a terrible role model."

My cousin is so jovial about this whole conversation that I feel certain this is not a bone of contention between Georg and his wife, Pam. It's great that he found someone who is a good fit.

"You know," Georg says in between his sets. "You should be careful here. I think there is something in the water. Evan met his wife here and they have a couple of kids. I met Pam here. And now even that *govnyuk*, Viktor, found someone to fall in love with him here. They have a baby on the way, as well."

"She must be a saint, his wife."

"Oh, they are not yet married," Georg gossips. "He knocked her up before they could plan the wedding. Scarlett says he passed out cold when she told him. She also works for the Crush in the PR department, doing social media mostly so you'll meet her soon. Pam and Scarlett are close, so we hang out as couples sometimes, but Viktor is still very much the Mad Russian fucker we all love to hate on the ice. Now that we are all on the same team, he is much more tolerable thanks to his little family, if you know what I mean."

I can't help but smile at the thought of big Viktor Demoskev fainting when he found out he was to be a father. It even elicits a slight chuckle as we switch to the cable machine for leg lifts. Georg grabs his water jug—yes, a giant jug of water, not just a normal-sized bottle—and holds it up before taking a chug. "I only bring my own water from home, now. Taking no chances on this baby-making issue."

"I would not mind being a father," I say as I adjust the Velcro ankle strap and check the weights. "If I found the right woman, that is."

"Well, there are plenty of women in this town willing to plead their case to a successful athlete."

I make a noise of distaste. "I am not interested in women like that."

"No?"

"You know me," I say, rolling my eyes. "Random women who just want to score an NHL player for the night will never appeal to me."

"Oh yes, I forgot you're a serial dater and boring as hell."

"Meh." I give a shrug. "So what if I'm boring?" He's not wrong. I *am* a serial dater. One woman at a time, even though I've been single for more than a year. I've had a few relationships over the years that were casual, but I'm finished with the one-night hookups that used to tempt me. Lately, those have been few and far between. The jersey chasers were always just so terribly fake—and still are, for that matter. Whenever I do take a woman to bed, I like to pick someone who doesn't follow hockey, who won't come looking for me later. I've been careful and kept my personal life private over the years. What happens behind my bedroom door is nobody's business. Playing the "I'm a boring guy" card has worked pretty well for me keeping my private life running smoothly under the radar. And that's just the way I like it.

"I think you might be a closet romantic," Georg says shaking his head at me. "There are so many fish in the sea. So many tasty, tasty fish for a single guy who looks like you."

"Do you regret settling down?" I divert the topic back to him once again.

"No, not at all. Pam is perfect for me. I think I knew it the first night we met."

"Now who is the romantic?"

"For her, I totally am."

"Well, then you understand what I am looking for. I don't need many women. I need the right woman. I just need one. And I will find her eventually. I can be patient."

"Finding the right woman can be life-changing," Georg admits. We finish up our workouts as he peers up at the clock. "Speaking of which, I'm supposed to meet Pam for lunch soon."

Georg leaves me shaking my head in disbelief as he takes off for the showers. It's hard to believe that any woman could have had such an effect on Georg Kolochev. He was truly wild when we were together in Sochi for the Olympics. Drunken, sex-crazed, and one hundred percent wild. His wild lifestyle mirrored his wild style of play on the ice. I was certain he would burn out early, yet here he is, thriving, married, and sober. *Or maybe, he was sober, married, and thriving.*

I stick around the gym to finish off with jump rope and box jumps before finally grabbing a quick shower and my bag to wander out into the searing hot Vegas afternoon. I will have to get used to the desert heat of living here full time. I'm thankful my apartment is only a few blocks from the practice arena so I can walk there in just minutes. The arena on the Strip where we play our games is about two miles from where I'll be living so I can just order an Uber to games if I don't want to do the longer walk in the heat wearing a suit. Which honestly doesn't sound too great.

But it does mean I don't need a car immediately, which is good since I sold mine when I got the trade from Austin. I had to have a car there, because everything was spaced out far and wide in the Texas landscape. The Comets arena and the practice facility were many miles apart. Neither were in the downtown area of Austin where I lived, but here in Vegas, everything is quite close, so I can manage on foot, at least for now. I'll probably have to get a car eventually when I find a more permanent place to settle. Scott told me that most of the players own homes in Summerlin, a town about fifteen miles outside of Vegas, where the environment is that of a regular family community, totally opposite of the hopping nightlife Las Vegas is famous for. I'll have to check that area out whenever I'm ready to look for a permanent home to buy. It's going to have to be somewhere much quieter than the Las Vegas Strip, that's for damn sure.

MY APARTMENT here is just a one-bedroom place that Scott helped me get into temporarily, smaller than my place in Austin, and nothing special. Despite my fat contract with the Crush, I'm just not doing as well financially as I could be. I mean, I haven't gotten a paycheck on my new contract yet, so that's part of it, but I had a decent deal in Austin and I'm not a baller by nature. My life is simple, and I don't spend money frivolously. I haven't taken enough interest in what my fund manager has been doing, or what he's invested in, but as I've looked over my most recent financial statements, I don't feel my investments are performing as they should be. If I'm reading them correctly that is.

And that's *the* problem. I have trouble deciphering numbers. Words too, but numbers are worse. The figures on the page might as well be hieroglyphics, the way they jump around and blur on the page in front of me. Basically, I can't interpret the annual statements. My fund manager is in Russia. With a little pit of anxiety welling in my stomach, I look at the clock. They are eleven hours ahead, so it's about midnight there. They're probably asleep. They've managed my money since I was much younger and

I'm still not doing as well as I should be, so maybe it's time to have an American advisor take a look.

I call Scott and explain I'm not the best at deciphering investments and strategy, and that my new contract is big enough but I'm concerned about it not being invested well with my current portfolio manager.

"Do you know anyone who could take a look at things for me?" I ask.

"Actually, yes, I know just the person for you to see. I'll shoot you a text."

4

# no nathaniel here

Talia

"How's the weather in Los Angeles today?" I ask my client by phone. And then a second time, since he's elderly and hard of hearing. "I said, how's the weather out there today?"

"Oh, just fine, just fine," he says. "Praying for rain as usual. You? You're where now?"

"Las Vegas. Harold moved me to build the sports business here."

"Sports, shorts," Mr. Riddle says. "Live fast, die young when it comes to longevity. Making money in sports is no good long-term strategy. You know what's been a good long-term strategy for me?"

"If I had to guess, I'd say you did pretty well in utilities and energy."

"Utilities and energy," he says, as if I didn't just say that exact thing.

"Right, you've done very well there, that's for sure.

Hey, Mr. Riddle, do you like the package I drew up for this next wave of investments?"

The little bell on my office door rings as it opens. I'm not expecting anyone, so I don't look up right away, figuring it's just a delivery person. However, when I do look up, I'm slightly taken aback. Enough so that I lose what I was about to say to Mr. Riddle, who is still babbling on about utilities and energy. I manage a fund—

"Can I call you back, Mr. Riddle?" He agrees, so I hang up, desperately trying to remember if I got that lunch lettuce out of my teeth from earlier.

The man in front of me?

Hulking. Huge. And not terrible on the eyes. He's got short, dark hair and a sexy five o'clock shadow. He's in jeans and a T-shirt—a T-shirt that's clearly been well-loved as it clings to his muscular frame, filling out his bicep region quite magnificently. An impressive, colorful tattoo snakes down one arm. It might even be a snake. Or a dragon maybe?

I'm not going to lie—I find him very, very attractive.

Yes. I. Do.

Which is very bad, because I promised myself, I wouldn't do this again. I would not think sexy thoughts about clients ever again after what happened in San Francisco.

He bites his bottom lip like he's nervous or shy or something and I realize I've been ogling him for like a minute now. Unprofessional much?

*Not a good start.*

"Hi." I clear my throat. "Sorry. I wasn't expecting anyone today."

"Should I come back?"

*Oh good Lord, he's got a super sexy accent. Okay, take a deep breath and get your shit together. He's probably not a client, and just here to deliver something.*

"No," I say, managing to get out of my chair. "How can I help you?"

"Scott Rose said Harold said to come here."

"Oh. Oh, okay." Scrambling around the desk, I move the box that once *again* occupies my lone guest chair. After the box is on the floor, I gesture that he should sit. He looks at the chair, then at me, as if he's unsure he's in the right place. Honestly, I get that a lot with new clients. I look too young and they think I can't possibly be the person who will help them with their sizable fortunes, especially if they've already met Harold, who is the quintessential slick finance guy.

I run my hands over my crisp, white shirt and black pencil skirt and push my glasses up on my nose before holding out my hand. "I'm Talia."

"Boris Drăghici." Gods, his voice is sexy. "I'm looking for Nathaniel Wentworth."

A tiny laugh escapes my throat and Boris looks confused. "It's Natalia," I say. "That's me. I'm Natalia Wentworth."

Boris's look of confusion settles further onto his handsome face. "I thought you said your name was Talia?"

Tah-lee-ah. The way he says it, stretching out the syllables is really quite lovely.

"Natalia," I say, my voice stupidly breathless. "Talia for short. I promise you I'm the one you're looking for."

He meets my gaze, and for just a moment, there's almost surprise in his eyes. Surprise that disappears as he pulls his top lip through his teeth and looks away, his cheeks turning slightly pink. It's disarming; he seems genuinely shy. And don't forget hot. So very insanely hot.

"Have a seat?" I gesture again to the lone chair.

His name sounds so familiar, but I can't place it. I blame his good looks. They have scrambled my normally high-functioning brain. He obliges and I return to the other side of my desk, thankful to sit back down, thankful to hopefully talk numbers, a subject that will return me to an intelligent and *functioning* frame of mind.

"You seem young for a financial planner," Boris comments. He looks around the very boring office space. Beige walls. Brown tile floor. No art. Unpacked boxes scattered about. A half-eaten sandwich on top of the file cabinet. No doubt it's not only my age that's causing him to doubt my ability.

"I'm twenty-three, which is young by most standards. However, I graduated high school at sixteen and college at nineteen. Harold hired me as an apprentice right out of school and I've had my own portfolio of clients since I was twenty. I promise I know what I'm doing."

"I am…intimidated," he says with a half-smile. "Perhaps you are too smart to talk to me."

"No, never," I answer, smiling back. "What can I help you with?"

Boris sighs. "I just moved here from Austin, and—

"

"Hockey!" I exclaim. Boris tilts his head in question. "I'm sorry. I was trying to figure out why your name sounded familiar. You're a hockey player. Right?"

"Yes, I played for Austin and was traded to the Crush. I have an investment guy in Russia, but I am concerned my investments are not being well-managed. I have a larger contract here and I want to protect it, make sure it's working for me."

"Do you have many expenses, Boris? Do you need a lot of it to be easily liquidated?"

"No, not at all. I am living very simply at the moment. I just want to protect what I have. And also, for the longer term. We can never be certain how long a career in the NHL is going to last. It could be over tomorrow with a bad injury and I've been at this for a while now. I really hope to finish out my playing career with this team."

"Okay, well, you're in the right place." I smile at him encouragingly. "Do you have any of your current investment paperwork with you?"

He shakes his head. "I wasn't sure what you would need and thought I'd just stop in to talk for a moment. Everything is at my apartment. Can I get my papers and take you to dinner to talk about it?"

Not what I was expecting.

A dinner invite from a potential client.

A smoking hot potential client, I might add.

*Shit.*

I can't accept his invitation. Can I?

*Did I mention he's fantastically beautiful* and *he needs my help?*

# 5
# very perky indeed

Boris

*hit.* Talia's mouth is hanging open in surprise. I wonder if she thinks I'm being inappropriate.

"I hope I have not offended you," I say quickly, trying to smooth things over. "I don't cook, and I just moved here. I thought maybe we could eat and talk because I skipped lunch today, and I don't really know the city yet…I feel kind of dumb eating by myself."

I must sound like such an idiot, babbling on like this to her. *Govnyuk.*

Talia blinks and then says, "I'm not at all offended, Boris. I'm also new to Las Vegas. I haven't figured out the single-appropriate restaurants yet, either."

"Oh, yes. Good."

She checks her watch and says, "I have a few calls to make, but if you come back at seven, we can walk somewhere nearby. Bring your statements."

I rise from the chair and hold out a hand, which she shakes before turning back to the computer, peering through her thick, dark frames, and picking up the phone. I guess that means this meeting is over for the moment, so I thank her and head for the door.

ON MY WALK HOME, I think about this Talia Wentworth. First, Scott definitely wrote Nathaniel, right? Or did I read his text wrong and just assume it would be a man? Maybe it autocorrected to Nathaniel when he typed Natalia. It wouldn't be the first time that's happened. But she's so young, just twenty-three. How can someone so young be representing the many millions of dollars that athletes make each year? She seems competent, though, and certainly seemed to know what she was talking about. Still, this is a big contract and I'm worried my personal investments are falling way behind where they should be. I really need someone who is a pro at this, so I call Scott back.

"Hey, man, I hate to bother you again, but you said Nathaniel Wentworth, right?"

"No, sir. Natalia. She's female," he answers.

"Did you know she's only twenty-three?"

"I know she's young, Boris, but I promise she's a top dog. Harold swears by her, calls her a genius. She comes highly recommended. Don't sweat it."

"Okay, then. She seems smart—"

"She is. Just give her a shot."

I thank him and hang up, then decide a shower is probably in order. I change into a green Polo dress shirt, rolling the sleeves up to my forearms, dark jeans, and a pair of soft leather loafers. I don't pay a ton of attention to fashion, but I think I look presentable. I gather my financial papers and shove them in a folder and then head back out to walk the few blocks to her office again.

She's on a call when I get there; talking a mile a minute about how the market is very volatile right now. "I don't know of any sure bets in the stock market right now, sir, but I agree this one seems solid for the long term," she's saying. She looks up and holds up a finger to let me know she'll be a minute. I wander to the window and look out at the setting sun to the west. Right at my feet are open file boxes. I see names of several pro athletes. Like, names you'd see in the news all the time. Very famous current athletes and ex-athletes. Scott wasn't kidding; if this young woman is working with these clients, then she really must be a financial whiz.

She finishes her call and I turn around, just in time to see her stand and knock a cup of coffee all over her white blouse.

"Shit!" She grabs a wadded-up napkin and tries to dab at it, to no use. "Well, at least it wasn't hot," she says annoyed.

"Do you have another shirt?" I ask.

"Do I have another shirt," she repeats, more to herself than to me. Then she smiles brightly and says, "Why yes, I do," as she comes out from behind the desk to root around in the box by my feet.

It's such a tiny office. Just barely room for her desk and chairs and a filing cabinet. Adding several unpacked boxes just makes it feel even smaller. And now she tells me to turn around so she can change her shirt. She's not a foot away from me and she's pulling off her white blouse right behind me. I don't know what to think. She's clearly oblivious to the danger this could pose to her if she were ever alone with the wrong person. I look out the window, but I can still see her reflection in it, now in nothing but a white, lace bra.

And surprise, surprise. I'm not dropping my eyes. I'm going to have a good look at what she's showing because, well, guy here. Like I told Georg the other day, I'm not a monk.

Her breasts are on the small side, but what they lack in size is made up for in perkiness. Her long legs are topped by a tiny waist that I could probably span with my hands. I thought she was just a numbers nerd with her big glasses and quick mind, but Talia is a lovely package. She's pretty and smart. Also, really fucking sexy with those perky tits that have grabbed my attention and won't let go. I don't know why I didn't notice how attractive she was when I met her earlier.

*Hold up just a minute.*

I should *not* be thinking about her this way if she is to be my financial advisor. This is a professional relationship.

"There," she says. That must be my cue to turn around. When I do, she asks, "Better?"

She has changed into a white T-shirt. It's got a V-neck and slim line that tucks nicely into her black skirt. It's barely different from what she had on before, just slightly more casual. I feel my face settle into a slight grin. Suddenly, all I can think about are those perky tits of hers and what they would look like without the damn shirt. I mentally kick myself back to a more appropriate line of thinking. She could be the answer to why I've felt something isn't adding up with my savings and investments. *Perhaps literally.* I can't come off as some horny weirdo.

"What kind of food are you in the mood for, Talia?"

*Hopefully, it's not shrimp.*

# 6
# life and stuff

Talia

I only come up to Boris's shoulder. He's truly massive, with wide shoulders and huge biceps. In profile, his straight-line nose and sensuous lips are really attractive so it's hard not to stare. Physically, he's masculinity personified, but I'm getting the impression his character is quieter, more reserved than I first thought. He's an interesting dichotomy.

"You know that I just moved here for a trade to the Crush." His hands are in his pockets, his shoulders just slightly stooped as his eyes flit toward me shyly. "What has brought you to Las Vegas, Talia?"

"My boss, Harold Shaw, asked me to come here and build his entertainment and athletic business. Vegas is a great market and we already had a handful of high-profile clients here. If I'm successful, we can grow our company."

"So just like that you picked up your life and moved?"

"I could ask you the same," I say.

"A trade is a trade. There is no choice in it."

"Well, I suppose not, unless you decide to go free agent."

"My contract was not yet eligible, but I am okay with it. I got a nice package to come here—better than Austin. Which is why I need someone to assist with my portfolio."

"I gotcha."

"But you did not answer my question, Talia."

Man, I love the way my name sounds coming out of his mouth. "Which one?"

"Your boss said go so you went? So easily? Didn't you have to leave friends or family behind?"

"Oh, that. Well, my family is in LA. And I was going through, um…some personal stuff back in San Francisco, so a move was actually welcome. Fresh starts and all, you know? Plus, it gives me a chance to show Harold I can build new business for the firm. It's a win-win for me."

"Twenty-three seems like very young for needing a new start," Boris observes. *Why is he so persistent? Is it because he's testing me?*

"Ah, well, you know. Life and stuff."

I literally cringe at how dumb that just sounded.

I'm nervous talking about this. I feel awkward and I keep running my hands over the front of my skirt as we walk. It's weird and I know it, but my hands are sweaty and gross. I mean, I can't just come out and tell this cute, new potential client (for whom I've already indulged in inappropriate and objectifying thoughts) that I moved here because I'm a home-wrecker. No, that would not be a good way to start things out, even if it's true.

*Why does he have to be so pretty?*

I remind myself to think of this dinner with Boris as if it's an interview. Is there any good way to spin the fact I left my last job because I slept with a client?

*Negative. It will probably never matter that I didn't know the truth...*

Ugh. I feel like I might throw up right about now. And why won't my hands stop sweating?

"So, you're from...Russia?" My voice is oddly squeaky, but the need to steer him away from asking about why I left San Francisco is imperative.

He shakes his head. "I was born in Romania. My mother is Russian, and my father is Romanian. My parents split shortly after I was born, we moved to Prague, in the Czech Republic. My mother and I moved again when I was twelve to return back home to her native Russia. I have lived in many places."

Of course, he has. In comparison, I lived at home until I was sixteen, then the dorms for all four years because I was too young for an apartment, and now I'm here. In a word, I feel underwhelming. *But he is fascinating.*

"How did you start playing hockey?"

"I always got in a lot of fights in school." He gives a somewhat apologetic shrug. It's kind of endearing, as if he's embarrassed about it. "My teachers suggested hockey to help manage my aggression. I did not do well academically, and it was frustrating, so I was always bad. Acting out in school helped to draw the attention away from my poor marks. At hockey I excelled though, and by the time I was a teenager I just wanted to quit school altogether. Thankfully, I was sent to an Olympic training facility shortly after. So really, hockey is what saved me."

"Wow," I say, not bothering to hide my utter fascination. "I can't even imagine how anyone would ever decide to willingly quit school. I loved school. Every minute of it. I'd like to go back for a master's degree at some point."

We stop at the entrance to a restaurant. It's got an Irish vibe, though Boris only looks at the menu posted at the entrance for a split second before looking off into the distance. I assume he doesn't like Irish food, so we keep walking, stopping at three more restaurants before I realize there is a pattern emerging. At this rate, I'll starve to death before any food appears on a plate in front of me.

"You want me to decide, Boris?"

He shrugs and gives me a sheepish grin. "I'll eat any kind of food. I don't need anything fancy, in fact, I'd be happy with a hamburger."

"Well, lucky for you, so would I."

I try to ignore the flip-flop happening low in my belly when his handsome face lights up with a warm smile and he nails me with his gorgeous brown eyes.

I do try.

Even if it's impossible.

# 7
# terrifying and sexy

Boris

I try my best to concentrate on the menu, but soon realize it's unnecessary when Talia begins to read aloud from hers.

"The garbage burger," she says excitedly. "Yummy. Avocado, tomatoes, mayonnaise, mustard, ketchup, onions, mushrooms. Sounds like heaven."

"Sounds maybe like a belly ache."

"Okay, how about the taco burger? Salsa, sour cream, taco chips, olives, onions."

"Onions again? Before our very first conversation about my finances? I don't think so, Talia." Teasing comes easily with her for some reason. And that is strange for me. Georg would be the first to tell people that I am serious and the most loyal person he knows...after I've eventually accepted someone into my world.

"Fine, killjoy. How about a classic cheeseburger with lettuce and tomato?"

The waitress comes with our drinks, a beer for Talia and an iced tea for me. She makes a face at my boring beverage choice and then rattles off her order, choosing the garbage burger without onions. However, she does order onion rings on the side, with a wink.

I shake my head and order the classic cheeseburger and French fries. When I look from the waitress back to Talia, she's got her head tilted, her eyes narrowed, and her lips set in a line.

"What?" I ask after the waitress has gone.

"Are you illiterate, Boris?"

My cheeks heat instantly. How perceptive this young woman is. And there is no judgment in her voice, only curiosity. She genuinely wants to know about me. I am beyond embarrassed. My first attempts to answer her come out in a lot of grunts and a shitload of *ahs* and *ums*. I bite my lip. My heart feels like it might pound out of my chest and start flopping around on the floor any second. *Fuck me.*

And then she puts an end to the torturous loop of my stuttering by speaking again. Thank sweet Christ.

"I'm just asking." Her voice is soft and kind as she looks intently up at me with her eyes, the color of the stormy sea. "I need to know so I can be assured that you have a full understanding of everything we look at together. If something takes more explaining, that's fine, but I don't want you in the dark if we're going to work together."

"I'm not," I say quietly.

"Not what?"

"Illiterate." I hate that word, even though I know she doesn't mean it in a derogatory way. "I can read, although not very well in English, as it is not my native language. My mother spoke in Russian to me from birth, so I learned that as well as being taught in Czech and English at school. It was never the speaking that was the problem for me anyway. It was the reading and the writing of the different languages that gave me so much trouble. But numbers? Forget it."

"Dyslexia?"

"Yes. Small print makes it worse. Numbers might as well be an alien language. They float and move, and I just can't get a handle on them. It's always been this way. Also, the reason I struggled in school so much, but I'm not dumb."

"I didn't think you were dumb. Not for a minute. But do you read your contracts before you sign them?"

"Usually no," I admit. "I'll set up a call and ask for an overview. I pretend I am busy and don't have time for a full review."

"So, you have advisors you trust, then? To ensure you don't get hosed?"

"Some," I say, though I'm certain I just winced a little and gave myself away.

Talia levels me, her blue eyes bright and insightful behind her thick eyeglasses. My heart continues its crazy pounding beat behind my rib cage. I feel like I'm on trial.

"So...your contract with the Crush?"

"Didn't read it," I say, taking a sip of my tea. "Got the highlights from my agent, Scott Rose."

"And your current investment strategist is in Russia?"

"Yes, in Moscow."

"Do you have a current contract with this guy?"

"No paper. It is a gentlemen's contract."

Talia sits back and huffs, rolling her eyes. "That is nuts, Boris. Seriously. Very risky. How much are they taking in commission and fees? What are they investing in? Are you at least looking at the numbers to see if the amounts go up or down each quarter? Are you making them review your portfolio with you periodically?"

I'm overwhelmed by all her questions. They are rapid-fire and her posture is just as aggressive as she sits forward, elbows on the table as she catches my gaze and refuses to let go.

Honestly, it's terrifying. But it's something else too —intensely sexy.

"I know the numbers are not where they should be, but they always tell me it's the markets and everything will rebound. I have worked with them a long time."

"Well, they've probably been ripping you off for a long time, then," she says sharply. Talia pushes up her glasses and then holds out a hand. "Here. Gimme. Let me see those reports."

I hand over the folder, and she proceeds to scrutinize each page, even pulling a pen out of her purse and making marks and circles. Her expression is intense at first, then changes. To something like shock or panic. *Oh shit.* She looks up and stabs me with dark eyes.

"Tell me."

"Boris, does your ass hurt? Because these guys are totally screwing you."

# 8
# bitcoin and blockchain?

Talia

Holy shit! This poor guy is getting screwed.

The more I look through these investment reports, the more I realize what a joke his financial "management" has been. Here's a professional athlete at the top of his career with his biggest contract to date in motion, and these shysters a continent away are nickel and dimeing him for every fee possible, making up reasons to siphon money from his accounts, and investing in the riskiest of risky bets. There is no friggin' way he could ever make his money grow over time in this situation. And if I had to guess, there's a river of green flowing right out of his accounts and into theirs. Because they think he's too stupid to catch any of it.

Damn, this pisses me off. Boris seems like a really good guy, who unfortunately has been royally taken advantage of, and probably for a very long time.

"Fuuuck." I push my glasses up on top of my head so I can rub my eyes. I guess I'm hoping if I rub hard enough, it will change what's on the page. No such luck, though.

"What is going on?" Boris looks concerned. Which is good. He should be concerned. I keep scanning as I talk.

"For one, these investments are all wrong. There's too much invested in big-risk endeavors like Bitcoin and Blockchain. And...holy crap, they put it in your IRA pool. Yikes. I mean, I know the Winklevii were all out strutting about making a shit-ton on cryptocurrency, but it's too high risk for a portfolio like yours. There could be money to make there, but the mining is intense and I assure you, your guys are not doing the work to make sure the investments are balanced with better bets, just to keep things even."

"I was told the higher the risk, the more I would make," Boris says.

"Yes, sure. I mean, higher-risk investments, when managed and balanced appropriately, can certainly net a higher rate of return. But they're risky for a reason, and they can kill your portfolio if no one is paying close enough attention. You do high risk, take the win, and get out. Reinvest in something middle-range for a while. And if you want to invest in higher risk anything, there are safer bets than cryptocurrency right now. There are some IPOs out there that are looking really strong. I can think of ten alternatives that would instantly give me less heartburn and would assuredly net you better returns than this bullshit."

Boris's mouth is hanging open. I think I broke him.

"You getting all this, big guy?" He nods and I nod back. "Good. Look, I need more time to look at this portfolio in depth and do a little research. Beyond Bitcoin, there are some highly irregular investments and I want to understand better why these choices were made. Is there someone I can talk to from your investment team?"

"Maybe Vlad?"

"Vlad is who?"

"He helps hockey players manage business that spans the US and Russia. He will know who you should talk to."

"So you don't have a direct line to these guys?" I'm sure the look of incredulity on my face isn't helping to ease his mind, so I try to soften my approach. I try the old standby of reminding myself that everything regarding money is fixable. In life, it's the stuff that money can't buy you really need to worry about.

He shakes his head. "They call me sometimes, but usually I get everything on paper in the mail."

"I'm sorry, but that's just shady as hell," I tell him just as the waitress brings our plates.

All this money talk has worked up an appetite. Seriously, this type of problem-solving is my jam, and I am totally turned on about the prospect of switching things around for Boris. I shove my giant garbage burger in my face, taking a huge bite and closing my eyes at the glorious flavors of condiments and vegetables with charred beef and a carb-tastic bun. I think I let out a moan that's borderline sexual.

When I open my eyes, Boris looks utterly enthralled. His own burger is perched in his fingertips, not a bite taken as he watches my display of gluttony. "You eat like a man," he blurts.

I crack up at this, but then look down and realize I've got a big glob of mustard right on my boob.

"Goddamn it! Fucking white shirts."

And Boris, the sweet angel, actually cringes.

"I'm sorry. I work with a lot of men who cuss a lot. It's an occupational hazard and certainly not very professional."

"It's okay," he says.

"You don't cuss?"

"Oh, I do, but usually just in my head. And not always in English."

This makes me laugh. The Ice Dragon is a contradiction. He's big and burly and plays a semi-violent sport, yet he doesn't drink, apparently, and he doesn't swear out loud. I wonder what he does to let off steam.

We finish our meal, talking about the tiny bits of Las Vegas we've experienced so far. When the bill comes, Boris offers to pay but I swipe the bill and promise it's an allowable business expense for me to take a potential client out for dinner.

"But I am making you meet after hours," he argues.

I'm not having it, though, and when I get my

business credit card out and hand it to the waitress, he pouts a little, his effort at chivalry thwarted.

Besides, what I don't tell him is that pathetic as it is, I work late every night and this was a welcome change having his excellent company for dinner tonight.

Yep.

PATHETIC.

And yes, the shouty caps are warranted.

# 9
# mr. honest engine

Boris

The general manager of the Crush is a goofy man. Bud Bellikowski is balding and wears what little remains up top in a comb-over. His striped polo shirt is clashing with the ill-fitting pants he's wearing, and his posture is terrible. But he does seem excited to have me on the team.

He pulls me aside to stand in front of the players who are now assembled in the locker room prior to our first official team practice of the season.

"This is Boris Drăghici," he says to the team. "AKA the Ice Dragon and the division's third-leading scorer last season. He's played four seasons for the Austin Comets and they were sad, sad, sad to see him go. But their loss is our win, and he's going to round out what I think is the strongest lineup this team has ever seen. Coach will talk more about this, but I think we'll run starting lineup with him at center ice and Evan and Mikhail on the wings."

"I think we need another Cold War so these

Russian players will stay on their own side of a lake," some young guy says. "Let us red-blooded Americans get some playing time."

Viktor Demoskev smacks the kid on the back of the head and says, "Shut up, asshole."

"Tyler, do you ever read the paper?" another player asks.

I try to keep my face neutral as I take a seat next to Georg, who says, "Tyler's a hothead with a big mouth but he's just joking. Demoskev's his BFF, so he doesn't actually hate Russians."

"It's okay," I respond. "I am not Russian."

"Marginally less Russian than I am," Georg argues.

"Very less Russian, cousin."

Georg just shrugs. We've played together most of our lives, in various capacities. It was fun to fill out the Russian team for Sochi together.

The coach stands up and talks about his expectations for this first week of practice, and for the season, before introducing Evan Kazmeirowicz. Evan is team captain and a very strong scorer.

"Hey, ladies," he says with a winning smile that spans the room before his eyes settle on me. "Welcome, Boris. It's good to see you. I think aside from when you played for the Comets, the last real interaction we've had was in Sochi. Is that right?"

I nod and give a half-smile. "I think so."

Evan gives a few notes and then sends everyone toward the ice. As I stand, he steps over and shakes my hand. "It's going to be great having you here with us."

"I am excited to be here, Evan. Really looking forward to working with the team."

"Awesome," he says. "Have you settled in okay? Sin City treating you well?"

"It has been fine. I am just learning my way around, still. How are you? Having a great career, and I hear you are married with children now."

"I think there's something in the water," Evan says with a laugh. "I got hit by Cupid's arrow and then Georg did, and then even that fool Demoskev. Watch out, or you'll be strung up soon, too. Though I will be the first to admit these women have made better men of all of us."

"That would be okay with me. First, I just want to play hockey, though."

Evan claps me on the back. "Good man. Hockey first, women second. Although I haven't heard those kinds of rumors about you."

"I'm boring that's why."

"Boring is just fine in life but not on the ice. See you out there."

He heads toward the door as I grab my stick and helmet. I stop at the water station to fill up my drinking bottle just to make a point to both Georg and Evan. They both laugh and shake their heads.

"Hockey first!" Evan repeats, grinning as we all head out to the ice.

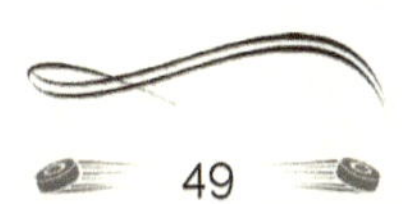

WE'VE DONE our full-team warmups and now are separated into skills training. I've taken about fourteen shots on goal when Coach tells me to take a break and head down to PT for a wellness-check on my late-season concussion. I switch out of my pads and boots and into a T-shirt, shorts, and trainers before heading down into the lower-level training and therapy areas. I wander until I find the PT space, a large room with about five individual therapy and massage spaces, some light equipment, a few workspaces, and a cryo-tub.

I'm greeted by a pretty blonde who says, "You must be the Ice Dragon."

"Boris." I hold out a hand.

She takes my hand and says, "Pam."

"Oh, nice to meet you, Pam. You are Georg's wife, yes?"

"Yes, though it depends on how annoyed I am with him on any given day whether I admit it."

I laugh lightly at her joke and she smiles, her eyes bright and twinkling with humor. I decide I like this Pam. I can see why Georg would make such life changes for her.

"So, my notes say you suffered a late-season concussion," she says, pointing me to a therapy table.

I climb on as I answer. "I did. It was nothing too serious but the hit was hard enough that I've had some ongoing pain in my neck and shoulders. It can cause headaches from time to time."

"Look at you, Mr. Honest Engine. Most guys

would not dare admit ongoing trauma, because they'd be worried about being benched."

"I want to play for a good many years, so I know I must take care of my body if I want it to last."

Pam smiles widely. "I'm going to put that on a poster for these other knuckleheads to see every time they come down here. I swear to God, these guys would come in here with their guts hanging out and be like, *'I'm fine. I can play!'*"

"I have been cleared to play," I remind her.

"I get that. I just appreciate your honesty. I can't help you manage pain if I don't know you're having it."

Pam does a standard concussion protocol and announces that she sees no lingering issues before having me lie down so she can work on the muscles in my neck, head, and back. It's probably been about six weeks since I last had the hands of a physical therapist work within my muscles. How did I forget how tight they were? How did I forget the sensation that even though it feels like my neck and back will be black and blue at the end, I'll have more range of movement back? And Pam is very good. She was the perfect PT with strong wrists and the ability to reach deep when mobilizing. *And fuck, at times it hurt like hell. Deep breaths, Drăghici.*

"So, Georg told me you're distantly related?" she asks as she works.

"Not too distantly," I say. "I am his father's cousin's son. So, his second cousin, I believe?"

"Did you grow up with him?"

"No, I was born in Romania and then moved to Czech Republic until I was a teenager, before moving again to Russia. We got to spend more time together once we were both training for the Olympics."

"And you played for Russia in Sochi?"

"Yes."

"He was a wild man back then, I hear."

"That is true."

"Come on, that's it?" she asks. "You're not going to give me the dirt?"

"A gentleman never tells such stories. They aren't mine to tell."

"Well, there aren't that many gentlemen out there anymore, I'm afraid. But good for you. I'm going to tell all my single girlfriends to get in line for you."

"No, no," I say. "I will find the right woman when the time is right. No set-ups, please. I will keep drinking the water here, though, just for luck." I give her a wink.

"Something tells me you're not going to need any luck, Boris, once word gets out about you." She gives me a wink back.

# 10
# or he's really a saint

Talia

The alluring scent of Chicken Lo Mein fills the tiny office as I try to eat and work. I skipped lunch and it's nearly eight already. My stomach is very angry with me.

It's been a busy day of calls and research and I still haven't gotten my files unpacked and organized. Nor have I had a chance to investigate further into Boris Drăghici's financials.

I pull out his folder and dig in, my notebook at the ready. I already know we're going to need to chuck the cryptocurrency from his portfolio, but as I scan the details, I see even more risky investing. There is money tied in options and futures, and even in exploratory drilling contracts throughout Russia. I note seven highly risky investment lines that will immediately need to be moved to standard-risk portfolios.

It gets worse as I go, though. Over the course of a year, I can see ten withdrawals not tied to a reinvestment strategy. They're not fees, though there are plenty of those and they are steep—a whole other issue that needs addressing—but rather, just amounts which got pulled from the portfolio and never reinvested. After talking with Boris, I don't think he's authorizing these large withdrawals. He doesn't strike me as someone who lives lavishly. Some of our foreign players support family in their home countries, and I guess it's possible he moves money to family, but the pit growing in my stomach says otherwise. The withdrawals are well-hidden enough so I doubt Boris would ever notice them. Considering his dyslexia and admitting he avoids reading as much as possible, I can't imagine he's even looking at all—and his investment agents are probably banking on it. *Literally.* But I'm so pissed off. From what I know of Boris Drăghici, he's a gentleman, not an asshole. Wish I could punch the lowlife scuzzballs who have been doing this to him.

I pick up the phone and call Harold.

"What's up, young pup?" he answers. "Doing any sinning in Sin City?"

I laugh and shake my head. "Doing lots of working for sure."

"That's my girl. Always looking out for the company. What's going on?"

"You know the guy you sent me? Boris Drăghici?"

"The Ice Dragon. Yes, ma'am. He's got a fat new contract out there. Did you get him on our rolls?"

"Nearly," I say. "But his prior investments have been managed overseas and there is just red flag after red flag as I'm looking through his numbers. This guy has invested most of what he's made and yet he's making nothing. He's losing big time, and I don't want to see him get hosed on this new multi-million-dollar contract with the Crush."

"Walk me through it."

I give him everything I'm seeing and support my thoughts with corresponding solutions. Harold listens and gives feedback but announces my plan is sound. "However, you've got to get the accounts away from his current investment agents first."

"Yeah, that's the second thing I wanted to ask about. Have you heard of a Vladimir Nechaev?"

"He's an agent-slash-fixer. A little gray, if you know what I mean," he says wryly.

Gray, in our world, means not totally good but not totally bad.

"I do know what you mean," I say. "My Spidey senses are going crazy on this one. Boris told me this guy Vlad could maybe get me in touch with his fund managers in Russia."

"Well, Vlad is a man who can make connections, yes."

"Is he Boris's agent?"

"No, that's Scott Rose."

"Oh," I say, breathing a sigh of relief. "Thank God. Boris is a good guy and he deserves a straight-up agent. Boris doesn't even read his contracts. He leaves it to Scott, so I'm glad to know someone principled has his back there, at least."

"Vlad's not bad, per se, he's out for the best

interests of the players he represents for the most part. He represents Viktor Demoskev, so there's another Crush connection if you need it. I suppose he's worth a call and you gotta start somewhere."

Harold and I talk about a couple of other clients and then say good night. We're two peas in a pod, Harold and me. We never stop working and we always win for our clients. I got really lucky having him for a mentor at such a young age. A timely internship in San Francisco while at uni got me in the door with his firm, and we hit it off from there.

As I inhale the rest of my now-cold noodles, I ponder what the hell this Vlad guy has to do with anything. He doesn't represent Boris, and he's not Boris's financial advisor. I mean, why can't I just call up these guys and talk to them like any normal businessperson would? So weird.

Still, when I get a text from Harold with Nechaev's cell phone number and a confirmation he's in the US, I automatically dial and hope for the best. He answers on the first ring.

"Hi, Mr. Nechaev?"

"Yes, this is Vlad Nechaev," he answers in a deep, heavily accented voice.

"I'm Talia Wentworth. I work for Harold Shaw and Baseline Investments. We're in the process of working with a new client whose investments have long been managed overseas. I was told to call you in hopes of having you connect me to the current investment manager for Boris Drăghici. He's got a new contract going here in Las Vegas and wishes to move his investments to a local investment manager."

"I have not heard this directly from Boris," he says after a lengthy pause.

"I'm happy to have him give you a call to confirm. I have to confess. I'm unsure of your role in this process. Honestly, I have a lot of questions for the investment manager that would better be discussed directly. I'm concerned, as is the client, why there has been so little growth and return after so many years." *Although, I know exactly why.* "If you could give me the contact details, I can make the call myself." *Nice one, Wentworth.*

Vlad laughs on the other end of the line. "I suspect maybe that the reason his investments are no good is because he isn't the brightest bulb in the lamp." *What the fuck?*

"That's not funny," I say flatly. "Mr. Nechaev, I don't have any idea why, in seven hells, I would have to go through someone with no direct connection to the client in order to have a simple business discussion. I just need to know who to call. Stop being an obstructionist to what is a totally normal business practice. What the hell do you have to do with any of this anyway?" *Here's hoping Mr. Condescending doesn't disconnect the call after that moment of unprofessionalism.*

I hold my breath for a moment, but then God bless him, this guy laughs into the phone yet again. "You are a real spitfire, Miss Wentworth. Look, I help players to straddle the United States and Russia.

Sometimes there are accusations about doping that we manage through independent drug testing. Sometimes we have visa and border issues. I do actual contract and player management as ninety percent of my business, but I am also known to help these players when they have business spanning the two countries. In this case, I am the conduit to the Ice Dragon's financial managers."

"Why the hell wouldn't they just talk to him directly? If I made my clients go through an intermediary, they'd say I was shady as hell and to fuck on off. This is beyond stupid. Just connect me so I can switch the accounts to our management, and I'll leave everyone alone after that."

"What a mouth on you," Vlad says, sounding delighted by my outburst. "Okay, because you are so ballsy, I will make a call for you."

"Thank you, I guess?" Christ, this is weird. "Please explain I'll expect to hear from them within the week."

Vlad offers some pleasantries and then we hang up, with me unsure of whether I should be pleased with myself, or worried. I think I feel a little of both. Yes, I do have a mouth on me, and perhaps I shouldn't blame it on my environment I worked in. But Vlad sounded far too cocky for me, and I wanted him to know I was serious. *Although, I've never heard Harold say fuck to a client's contact. Shit.* Oh well, time will tell. Hopefully, I didn't just shoot Baseline Investments in the proverbial foot.

The last call I make for the night is to Boris. He

sounds sleepy when he answers, but I ask him if he can pop in the office for a quick update sometime this week. He says he'll check the practice schedule and stop in when he can. I mention he may need to call Vlad Nechaev to let him know he does indeed want to move his investments to an American investment manager. I'll also have paperwork for him to review and sign in order to start the process. When he hesitates, I immediately promise to assist him with the contract review...preferably in the presence of someone he trusts, like Scott Rose, but keeping Scott blind to the reason *why* he's needed there.

He thanks me and says good night in that sexy accent of his which should be illegal. I seriously doubt he's even remotely aware of his hotness.

I can't stop thinking about Boris Drăghici on my short walk home from my office, so much so that I settle on my chaise and pull open my laptop to do some reconnaissance, rather than my regular habit of opening a book to read. LuLu even complains loudly at being displaced by the evil hard metal thing taking up *her* spot in my lap. I'm forced to set her up on the gray blanket tucked in beside me before I can even get started.

It's funny. When I take on a new client, I usually avoid most of the tabloid gossip. And there is always tabloid gossip. Models, drugs, drinking, partying, violent behavior, car accidents...whatever. There's always something, and sometimes stuff turns out to be true. Usually, it has zero effect on my work with the client, unless the true stuff ends up costing money that needs to be liquidated. Still, I'm not the judge or jury, and my job is always to make the most of a client's investments. That is all.

So imagine my surprise when I see *nothing* incriminating about Boris Drăghici. Anywhere. There are profile articles about his training in Russia, about the fact he was chosen to play in the Sochi Games after only two years of full-time training. He warmed the bench, but stayed in training and ended up starting in the Sochi games four years later. The only child of divorced parents, he moved with his mother back to her native Russia when he was twelve. He played Russian league throughout his career and then was picked up by Austin four years ago on one of the best rookie contracts in the league. His deal with the Crush is based on several solid years of scoring domination, and it's almost better than Crush golden boy, Evan Kazmeirowicz.

I keep hearing rumors Evan may retire soon. He's got a family now and he's not as young as he used to be. He's still an ace on the ice and he's a strong winger to Boris's center position. They'll make a good pair, a strong pair, but there's a lot of pressure on Boris, who is here for one sole reason: to bring the Crush another championship season.

The articles are all focused on his power, his speed, and his ability to avoid the spotlight. He's mostly described as shy, introverted, and low drama. There are no photos of him with half-naked women, no pictures of him partying. I even check the WAGs (Wives & Girlfriends) page for the Austin Comets to see if he was ever linked to anyone. Nope. Boris Drăghici is listed as one of the few "single" guys on the team. Which isn't unheard of, really. There are always players who manage to keep their private life just that. Or they're gay, and solidly in the closet. Pro sports makes it really hard to be out and proud, sadly. Having social media accounts for the public to stalk is rule number one. And Boris doesn't have Facebook, Twitter, Snap, or Insta that I can find. Lots of dead searches for information about him are out there though. So, there *is* a curiosity about him, but with no picture evidence to speculate about, it doesn't go anywhere.

Everything I could find is focused on him as an athlete or as a member of the Comets. There's a cute *Weird Hockey* clip of him being asked which celebrity he's been told he looks like. He replies innocently, "No one looks like me." The adorable smile on his face as he sits perched atop a tall stool in his perfectly tailored suit has me captivated. Boris either has excellent media management or he is legitimately a saint.

I do find a handful of marketing photos from his time with the Comets. There are some "sexy" photos of the team out there, shirtless photos. And Boris is... well, he's kind of perfect. I stare at the images for a long time, taking in the sparse dark hair on his perfectly sculpted pectorals. His washboard abs lay a trail down into unbuttoned jeans in one shot. His tattoo, a colorful dragon that curves from shoulder to wrist, only accentuates his bulging biceps. And that face. Holy crap. Piercing eyes. Perfect lips. Stubble that makes me want to—

Nope.

*Stop it, Talia.*

You cannot get naked with another client. Not after what happened in San Francisco.

I click out of my Google search and sit back, eyes closed, trying to will my hot-and-bothered body to calm down. I went down the rabbit hole with those pictures of half-naked Boris, which I shouldn't have done. Wasn't it a gross invasion of privacy? *Negative. He's too gorgeous to be ignored completely.* How will I even be able to look him in the eye knowing I was like minutes away from needing a vibrator session with him in mind?

I take a deep breath. And then, just to remind myself of how a poorly made decision turned out for me in the past, I go to Facebook and look up Cameron Thompson. Cameron Thompson, with his model looks and perfect, panty-melting smile. Cameron Thompson, with a wife and three adorable children. Cameron Thompson, who was married when I slept with him. Five times.

Cameron keeps his profile public, which is insane for a person as wealthy as he is. He's thirty and a Silicon Valley tycoon already, married to his high school sweetheart.

The first time I met him at a client meeting, there was a chemical reaction. I felt it and I was uncomfortable about it. But weeks later, when he called me to confirm if I was feeling what he was feeling? It was like two magnets pulling us together. The next time we met for dinner to discuss his investments, we ended up screwing in his car. Then there was the *all-night software development crisis* where he took me to a hotel. Hmmm.

Those overnights happened five times before his wife came to my office and called me out in front of Harold and one of our baseball superstar clients. She called me a home-wrecker and a gold digger and several other names that don't bear repeating. I tried to explain I had no idea he was married. We'd only ever talked about his investments, never about family, and he never wore a wedding band. When she stormed out of the office, I was left red-faced with a sick pit in my stomach—I was *not* that woman who would ever sleep with a married man—and I was also sure Harold would fire me posthaste.

He didn't, though. Instead, he told me "shit happens" and that I "made a rookie error in judgment." And he then told me I was to go build Baseline's Las Vegas client base.

As I take in the smiling photos of Cameron with his pretty wife and cute kids, his lavish life on boats and at charity events, I feel disgusted. With myself. But also very angry at Cameron for not only what he did to me, but what *he* did to his undeserving family. *God, I hope I'm the only one he's done this with.* I slam my laptop shut, angry I let myself be so dazzled by him. I can't do it again. *I won't do it again.* I'm going to stay focused on my work and my business. If I can do that, everything will be just fine. *If only I'd done a*

*Google search on Cameron...why didn't I? Why didn't I look up these details? He wasn't shy of media attention, so why did I not know or check?* These are the questions I have asked myself ad nauseam. Funnily enough, I never get past the answer of, *You loved the unexpected and extremely stimulating attention and your reason went out the window.*

Boris can be my *imaginary* lover tonight. My muse. I pull my trusty vibrator from the small wooden box I keep under the chaise and remind myself there are plenty of hot, fictional characters to imagine.

It'll just have to be enough for me right now.

# 11
# welcome to the crush

Boris

"You look a little...constipated," Scarlett says with a giggle. Her cheeks turn pink against her alabaster skin as she grins at the images when they pop up on the computer screen to be edited.

"That doesn't sound good," I comment.

"Nope, not the look we're going for. And I know you can do better because I saw those sexy pictures you took for your last team. Your Crush pics need to be at least as nice."

"I had hoped those had gone away by now," I say, cringing.

"We are all immortal on the interweb."

"So it seems. They were very adamant that sexy photos would help with attendance."

"Did it work?"

"I believe so. Certainly not just because of me, though."

"Uh, whatever," she answers, rolling her eyes.

"Have you looked in the mirror lately? You're hot. You could probably get a woman pregnant just by looking at her." I laugh. *What the hell?*

"Scarlett, what have we talked about?" Sid, her photographer scolds jokingly.

"Sorry. Inappropriate. Got it."

Scarlett Woods manages most of the Crush's social media and public relations. She's got the perfect name, since her hair is long and red and her personality is fiery. She's curvy, with large breasts and ample hips, and the slightest hint of a baby bump protruding under the cloth belt of her dress. She rests her hand there protectively as she stands back to let the photographer take a few more pictures. A glittering diamond adorns her ring finger. This is who Georg mentioned, so she must be Viktor Demoskev's fiancée.

"You are the woman who tamed the beast," I comment, changing the subject away from my apparent hotness. "Viktor's fiancée, correct?"

She grins. "He's a beast all right. And yes, we are now engaged and expecting a child because why not just do everything all at once?"

I laugh and the photographer tells me that was perfect. He allows me to slip off the chair to take a peek at the images and I now see what Scarlett meant about the previous photos. My smile was all wrong, awkward and weird. These new ones are much more natural.

"Those are perfect," Scarlett says, clapping the

photographer on the back. "Sid, my boy, you are a photography genius. I love ya."

"Well, headshots are not my forte but I'm glad these are working out okay," Sid says.

The photographer looks young. He can't have been doing this for very long, but I have seen some of his game day photos and he's very talented.

"Thank you for not making me look like a *pridurok*," I tell him.

"Um, you're welcome?" Sid answers.

"It means idiot," Scarlett says. "In Russian."

"I thought I read in your stats that you were born in Romania?" Sid asks, as he quick-edits one of the shots. "Scarlett, you want this in your inbox now, I assume?"

"Yup," she says. "Come on, big man. Let's go upstairs and get some questions answered for the next social media campaign. First question: Are you Russian or Romanian?"

"I was born in Romania, my father's country, but lived in the Czech Republic until my early teens. After my mother and father divorced, she chose to return to her native Russia and I went with her to begin my training for Olympic hockey."

"That was concise," she says, laughing. She stands on tiptoes to kiss Sid on the cheek, thanking him before motioning for me to follow her out into the hallway. We walk to the elevators and take one to the administrative floor, where her office is located. She leads me to a conference room and asks if I need water or coffee. I turn down both, just ready to get this over with. I am not a fan of self-promotion, though I realize it is required of me.

Scarlett takes a seat opposite me and lets out a sigh, closing her eyes. "I'm only like five months along and already worn out. Imagine when I'm like three times this size."

She takes off her high-heeled shoes and then turns her attention back to me as she opens an iPad and taps her pen against it. "So, you played in the Sochi games for Russia, right?"

"Yes, I was on the official team." I played exactly one shift in those Olympics, but I don't need to tell her that.

"But not for OAR in the Korea games?

"No."

"Were you bothered by the fact that Russia could not be represented as a country?"

"Is this really part of your series?"

"No," she admits. "I'm just curious."

"I was not bothered."

"So you're, what, twenty-six?"

"Twenty-eight."

"And you've been playing in the US for four years?"

"Yes."

"You know, these one or two-word answers are not gonna cut it, buddy," Scarlett teases.

I lift a shoulder. "I'm not an exciting guy." *And you've only asked me yes or no questions so far.* But I know not to voice that out loud.

"You're exciting on the ice, as far as I can tell. Fast,

calculating. You're among the top scorers in the league. What makes you love hockey so much?" *Ah. Here is a better question.*

"Initially, hockey gave me a place to direct my teenage energy and frustration. It grew into something I was good at, so I put all of my focus toward it."

"There we go," she says, grinning. Her grin disappears from her face quickly, though, and she shoots to her feet. "I'll be right back."

Scarlett Woods literally goes running out of the room, a hand over her mouth, in her bare feet. I crane my neck until she disappears, then sit back, confused.

I'm playing a game on my phone when she returns a few minutes later.

"I'm so sorry about that," she says, shaking her head. "People tell me I'll feel better in the second trimester but that has not been the case for me."

"Oh, you threw up?" I ask, surprised.

"Profusely. I apologize."

"There is no reason to apologize. Pregnancy is a miracle, even those parts."

"That's awfully sweet. Viktor always looks like he might puke, too."

I just grin and shake my head. Scarlett asks why and I answer, "There is a common joke I have heard about something being in the water here. Players finding love with the women who work for the team, getting married, having babies. Though Georg says no way to children."

"Probably a good idea," Scarlett says with a laugh.

"How is this possible? Perhaps I really should go drink from the water fountains."

"You looking for love, Mister Ice Dragon?"

"I would not be opposed to finding love, but I want it to happen naturally, because I am not a man who is looking for something cheap."

"Well, if that doesn't make women swoon. I'm surprised they're not lined up outside the doors. But I will say that none of us came by these relationships easily. We all had baggage to overcome. The no-fraternization policy of the team being one." She chuckles and then adds, "It's probably time to ditch the policy now, anyway. It's kind of a joke after three players got involved with staff. And Max Terry is a big softie about it anyway."

"Oh, I am not looking to make any waves. My main priority is the game."

"Focused, determined, ready for what comes next," Scarlett says as she writes. "A pro at sixteen. An Olympian at twenty. A superstar in the KHL and then the NHL. And now you've brought that focus on the game over here to benefit the Crush. I like it."

We talk for a few more minutes before I announce that I need to get changed for practice. Scarlett thanks me for my time and walks me out, introducing me to her boss, Fiona, as we walk past a spacious office.

"So very nice to meet you, Boris," Fiona says, shaking my hand and holding it a little overlong. She wears a wedding ring but seems like a woman in need of attention from a man. Her eyes are the wandering kind. I've seen a few of those over the years, so I know what it looks like. I also know how to act oblivious and uninterested. Lots of practice.

I nod as Scarlett tells her boss that I'm the strong, silent type, which makes them both giggle, and makes me feel uncomfortable. I can feel my cheeks heating, so I thank them both and leave as quickly as possible.

The team is mostly dressed already when I enter the locker room, so I hurry to pull off my street clothes and shove myself into my practice uniform pants. I'm only a minute behind them as I take the ice, apologizing to Coach and letting him know I was stuck with the PR team. He pairs me with Viktor so I can practice shots on goal while Viktor practices defending the goal. What I don't understand is why he's brutally checking me hard, as if I'm an enemy and not a comrade. *What the fuck is wrong with him?*

"I met your Scarlett today," I say as I lob a shot that strikes the goal's corner post. Viktor skates to it, passes it back to me, and gets back into position. "She's quite vibrant. Glowing with your child. You are a lucky man."

I move with the puck, ready to make the shot when Viktor barrels at me. He checks me again, but this time, he pulls off his gloves and helmet and gets in my face, my practice jersey balled in his fists as he growls at me.

"What's your problem?" I ask, shoving him off me. "This is practice. I'm your teammate."

"Stay the fuck away from Scarlett," he hisses at me, teeth bared like an animal. "Do not look at her. Ever."

"Peace, brother," I say as he slams me into the glass.

Evan and Georg pull him away, Georg swearing a blue streak in Russian as Evan orders Viktor to the bench to cool off. Coach calls the whole lot of us over to the benches as Viktor skates to grab his gloves and helmet.

"You okay?" Evan asks me.

"Yes, I'm fine, it's okay." And it is. Viktor Demoskev didn't get his reputation for being a hothead from nowhere. And his fiancée is pregnant. He probably feels a lot of things, including protectiveness. And hockey players fight a lot. It's no big deal.

As we near the benches, though, Demoskev, still practically breathing fire, glares at me.

"Hey, Viktor, I meant no disrespect. Only making conversation."

"I can't believe you are among lead scorers," he bites back. "Hard to believe such a pussy would be successful in hockey."

Georg is up in Demoskev's face immediately. "What the hell is wrong with you? Get your head out of your ass. He's being nice, you fucking moron."

"Third best scorer in the league. Fifty-two goals in his rookie season. Olympic prospect at fourteen," says Mikhail, the winger who pairs so well with our team captain, Evan. "What are your stats, Demoskev? Leader of the dirtiest checks in hockey history? How many hours do you spend in the box each season? Back the fuck off the new guy."

Viktor's partner on defense, Tyler, chimes in next, "No one needed this asshole here anyway. Everything was good but ownership got greedy, and now we've got this hand job out here upsetting everybody."

Shouting breaks out between several of the players as I watch in disbelief. It's only when our coach whistles that things go silent. We all turn to face him for the ass chewing that's coming because he does not look pleased. "Grow the fuck up, you bunch of teenagers. What the hell do you think this is? A playground? No, it's a fucking professional hockey team. You all get paid a shit ton of money to do a goddamn job, not to fight like fucking bullies in the school yard."

A round of "sorry, Coach" ripples through the group.

"Yeah, well you're gonna be real sorry, now," he barks. "You ass-clowns get to do extra training hours until you can get along and play like a unit. I'm not having this level of bullshit out on the ice when we're in season, so get it out of your systems, or suffer the consequences. We're not missing out on the Cup this year. It'd be sheer stupidity if we did, what with a lineup like this. If we fire on all pistons, there's no reason we can't get there, so get your shit together and act like fucking grownups."

We're all quiet for a moment as Coach explains what he intends for us to do. Our punishment begins with some real remedial drills. The guys groan and most of them blame Viktor, who scowls the whole way through. When we have finished up and are in the locker room, the last thing I see of Viktor is his naked ass as he heads into the showers. His friend Tyler, however, holds two fingers up to his eyes, then points those fingers at me. He mouths, "I'm watching you," flips me off, and disappears into the showers, as well.

*The fuck?*

"Welcome to the Crush," Georg says, patting me on the back. "We're really glad you're here."

"Right. I'm feeling the love for sure."

# 12
# what hot librarian?

Talia

I finish a morning conference call with the San Francisco office and stand to stretch. I should take a walk or something. I swear it feels like I hardly get out of my chair some days.

There's a sticky note on my computer monitor that just says "Boris" with a question mark. It's my reminder that Boris was supposed to pop in to talk about next steps with his portfolio. It's been more than a week since I called him, and he still hasn't come by. I've tried calling but he doesn't answer, and his phone doesn't have voice mail set up. It annoys the OCD person in me, so I may have to set it up for him the next time we talk. Mind you, I'm barely hanging on by a thread with the lack of follow-up from *Vlad*.

You know, I'm not that far from the practice arena and I need to walk and find some lunch anyway. Maybe I'll just wander over that way and see if I can catch him at practice or something.

It's hot as hades when I step out into the highnoon sun. I'm thankful I'm just in a sleeveless dress and peep-toe shoes because otherwise, I might combust. There are tourists milling about, looking at lunch menus as I step by them. When the arena comes into view, I grab three hot dogs from a street cart and shove one into my face as quickly as I can right there and then, asking the vendor to put the other two in a bag for me. He comments on my intestinal fortitude and I thank him because my iron stomach is one of my finest virtues, in my humble opinion.

At the arena, I find the visitor's entrance. A security guard asks for credentials, which I don't have, and I manage to sweet talk him by telling him I'm Boris's girlfriend and that I've brought him lunch. Holding up the bag and giving him what I hope is a cute smile, he rolls his eyes and waves me through, telling me, "Next time, one of those better be for me." Men. Food and sex. It's always one or the other that makes them easy to persuade.

I grab a seat as part of the team heads off the ice. I see Boris out there with a smaller group of players. One of the coaching staff has them get into a circle and they start what looks like a pretty rudimentary exercise. Each one passes the puck to another in the circle, shouting out a name. It's very strange to watch and not at all what I'd expect from a pro-practice session.

The head coach stands on the outside of the ice, several rows in front of me, arms crossed over his chest. He's watching them intensely.

A blond guy smacks his stick on the ice and yells, "This is for babies!"

"Because you idiots all acted like babies," the coach yells back. "Add in a stat you know about the person you pass to."

I chuckle, pulling my second hot dog out to eat while they finish up, realizing I was right. This is rudimentary. But also, it seems, on purpose. The coach is making them do this for some reason, and I, for one, am quite intrigued about what they did to earn such a belittling punishment.

Practice ends maybe twenty minutes later, and as the guys head out and down the tunnel, I rush through the labyrinth of entrances and exits, trying to find the elevator that will take me to the locker room level. When I find it, a couple of guys are exiting, so I worry maybe I've already missed Boris.

The blond guy who yelled about the drill being for "babies" comes out as I reach the locker room doors. He looks me up and down and says, "You need some help? Lost?"

"I am looking for a player?"

"I'm a player." He grins, waggling his eyebrows at me.

"What I should have said is I'm looking for Boris Drăghici. I'm his financial advisor. Is he still in there?"

"Figures," he says, shaking his head. He opens the door, rolls his eyes and yells, "Hey, Ice Dragon, some hot librarian is out here waiting for you to wet her whistle."

Letting the door shut once more, the guy says, "I'm Tyler. Starting defense, just so you know."

"That's great?" I answer because I'm not sure why he's telling me this. "Do you need an investment manager?"

He leans against the wall, all tall and broad-shouldered, grinning at me. "I mean, we could roll around in money if that's what you're into."

"I, uh…" I make a face because this is just weird. "I think I'm good. But thanks."

He straightens and brushes past me with a shrug. "Just because he can score on the ice doesn't mean he can score in the bedroom."

All I can come up with is a lame, "Whatever."

A few minutes later, I'm still racking my brain, trying to think of something better than "whatever," when Boris steps out. He sees me and his eyes go wide.

"Hey there, champ," I say, probably too brightly. I feel weird and awkward. Which is nothing new, because I feel weird and awkward most of the time when I'm around people I don't know very well.

"When Tyler said a hot librarian was waiting for me, I wasn't sure what he meant."

"I, uh, well…" I stammer, trying to find any words as a possible response to his comment. "I'm, ummm, neither hot nor a librarian, so I'm not sure either. I told him I was an investment manager and he said something about, uh, rolling around in money. I mean, there was a time once that I thought I might like to be a librarian because I like to read a lot but once I learned about depreciating assets, I thought maybe libraries in their traditional sense might actually fall into that category. I mean, I love real books, don't get me wrong. I like the weight and the feel of turning a page. Oh, and the smell. Nothing like it. But really, e-books have effectively taken away the need for librarians in the traditional sense. As a financial analyst, I'd never allow a client to invest in traditional publishing, for example. I feel like librarians are a dying breed."

As I wind down, I realize poor Boris's eyes might look a little glazed over.

"Oh, God. I do this sometimes. Holy crap, did my senseless rambling make you malfunction? Sorry."

He blinks and gives me a glowing smile. "No, I found it fascinating."

"Really?"

"Yes, I mean, I don't read, as you know, so I never think about things such as libraries. You have. It's interesting to me."

I feel my lips pull into something like a wince or a cringe, because I'm sure he's just placating me. Most people let me babble and couldn't care less what my random brain is analyzing, unless it's something that can make them money.

"But you've probably figured out by now that I didn't come here to talk to you about libraries, Boris."

"Yeah, I know." He looks down at the floor before lifting his eyes back up to meet mine, with maybe the hint of a blush to his cheeks. *Oh Jesus, send help.* Blushes from this guy might just kill me dead if I don't exert some self-control over myself —stat.

"Do you want to take a walk?" I suggest.

"I'm headed toward home on foot, so sure."

We make our way out to street level and Boris pulls on a pair of sunglasses that raise his hot quotient by a billion. Gawd. I mentally give myself a head slap to remove all sexy thoughts from my brain so I can have a serious business conversation with him.

"You were supposed to come see me last week." I figure a gentle scolding is in order since he did miss an appointment.

He bites on his upper lip and gives a nod. "Sorry, yes. The team was not...ah—not working smoothly together as a unit. We are arguing a lot, so Coach Brown makes us have extra practice each day now to work on team cohesion."

A tiny laugh escapes my throat and when Boris looks at me questioningly, I say, "No wonder. I saw those junior league drills going on and wondered."

Boris just shrugs. "I don't mind though because I want to perform well for my new team. I'll do whatever is necessary to help us all work better on the ice together. This coach knows what he's doing. I have faith these drills will help."

We continue walking as I find myself thinking about how trusting Boris seems. How easygoing he appears. He's not the typical professional athlete, at least not among the hard-partying Crush players. I've seen the stories on PlayersBeingBad.com that detail the parties, the fights, and the general craziness that goes down behind the scenes of a pro sports team. Some of them have settled down, sure, but there are still plenty more who live up to Sin City's reputation to the fullest. The flirty defenseman Tyler who called me the "hot librarian" (thank you very much) comes to mind. But Boris doesn't fit that mold—not even a little. I continue to be astonished by how simply he seems to live his life, how easily he lets conflict just roll off his back. He must have *some* vices, right? A boy scout on the outside and a filthy animal between the sheets, maybe?

Of course, I could name myself as being that way (kind of), before I got burned.

Not that my drama has anything to do with Boris.

Nope, I'm not bitter at all. And I'm definitely not projecting my own issues onto this super nice gentleman, a pro-hockey hunk of a man.

*Who is my very professional client, and not a sex object, Talia.*

Oh geesh.

"So Boris, I've been thinking..." I give myself a mental slap to get my thoughts back in line.

"About?"

"Well, I think maybe your investment folks in Russia might be taking advantage of you. I'm not sure yet to what degree, but I've reviewed your investments six ways to Sunday and there's some really weird shit going on there."

Boris stops walking and looks at me, his mouth set in a frown. I can't see his eyes, so I'm not sure if this is a look of concern or anger, or where that anger would be directed.

"Are you suggesting my financial agents mismanaged my investments, or that they have stolen from me?"

"I'm, uh, not totally sure..."

"I think you are. Talia, I do not know you well, but I do know you are intelligent and perceptive. I have no doubt you have a very good idea of what has happened to my investments."

My mouth opens in surprise. I shut it and we start walking again. "I'm seeing some evidence of money being withdrawn from your portfolio and not reinvested. I see high-risk ventures which seem to be specifically chosen to explain away large drops in value. There seems to be double-dipping on fees. And the fact they don't let you call them whenever you need to, make you go through a middle-man like Vlad, it's just shady. They know you don't read contracts and you don't analyze the investment materials line-by-line. They expect you will simply trust them, and I think you're getting ripped off." He takes a few deep breaths and looks to the concrete, but I didn't miss the anger beneath the surface.

"Would you like to get coffee?" he asks, gesturing to a coffee shop. I realize we're now only doors from my office, and we could just go there, but I do love coffee, so I nod and we head inside.

After I order a double-shot latte and Boris orders his iced tea, we take a seat along a row of windows, Boris in his athletic shorts and T-shirt, looking very fit and his usual effortlessly sexy human. And me, the non-sexy librarian with, yet again I realize, hot dog mustard on the front of my pale blue dress.

I rub my forehead with my hand, trying to stop the headache that's suddenly blooming there.

"Are you okay?" Boris asks.

"Nothing a giant cup of caffeinated amazingness won't help." I salute him with my coffee cup.

"Okay, so I am sorry I did not come to visit you," he apologizes again. "It sounds as if you had plenty to share with me. It's just I spend a lot of time at the arena with physical therapy and practice sessions."

"It's okay, Boris, I totally get it. I'm probably very low on your priority list as you're settling in."

"No, not true. My financial situation is quite important to me, as my new contract is in play and I don't want to lose more than I already have. I came to you for help, Talia, and I'm just sorry I haven't been able to get back to you sooner."

I consider him for a second. "So, I had a crazy idea."

"Which was?"

"Maybe we can hire you a part-time assistant? Like, someone to manage your calendar, organize your bills, prioritize things for you? Just, maybe, ten hours a week. The person can take calls for you, set appointments, you know…help keep you organized?"

"I don't think that's necessary."

I fold my arms over my chest and stare him down. He takes a drink of his tea and looks out the window.

"Look, Boris, people are taking advantage of you.

It's important we have someone looking at all angles of your life to make sure it doesn't continue to happen. Getting you help you need is a first start. I can help you find the right person, someone you can trust."

"I trust you," he says quietly, still looking out at the sidewalk traffic going about their Las Vegas business as usual.

This warms my heart, but it's not enough. "That's awesome, so trust me now when I'm saying that I think this is a good first step in getting your finances on track."

One corner of his mouth puckers, a sign he's considering my idea. Finally he sighs, and focuses back on me, a half smile on his handsome face. "Okay, Talia. If you think it will help, I will give it a try."

"Great. I'll do a little digging and find some folks for us to interview together. I promise this will be really good. And it will make me feel better to know someone is looking out for you."

Boris nails me with his chocolaty eyes and asks, "But who looks out for you, Talia?"

My breath catches in my throat, and it takes me a second to bring my shorted-out brain waves back online.

I manage to steel myself enough to say, "*I* do."

Even though I know it's a lie.

# 13
# shower dreams

Boris

Talia's office is so small. Too small, really. I feel like a bull in a china shop, especially since Talia still hasn't unpacked the boxes upon boxes of files stacked all over the place.

There's still only the one extra chair, and it is home to a large stack of said files at the moment. So when the second candidate that Talia has chosen to interview for this position she thinks I need comes in, there's still nowhere for the candidate to sit. The first interviewee was clearly very thrown by the not sitting, and paced nervously the whole time.

This candidate, however, looks around and says, "What a cramped space. I'm Ally. Well, Allesandra really, but I go by Ally."

Talia shakes Ally's hand. "Yes, well, maybe the next position I fill will be for a person to help make this space more functional. Let me introduce you, however, to Boris Drăghici. He's a new center for the

Crush, just moved here from Austin, and in need of someone to help manage his calendar, bills, and calls."

Ally, to my surprise, shakes my hand and then begins moving files around. She starts with the chair, grabbing the whole stack of files and moving them to the file cabinet along the wall. She peers at the boxes and then starts moving things into more permanent homes. All the while, she talks.

"I hope you don't mind," she says. "I'm a little OCD and my mind just automatically goes to organization. I won't be able to focus until I've done this, and hopefully it will help you have a more functional office space, regardless of whether I get the job or not."

I look at Talia, unsure if this is good or not good. Talia wears a small, sly smile, as if she purposely left the files on the chair to see what people would do. I can suddenly see the design of this, the purpose for leaving her office so disorganized. She wants a self-starter. And Ally seems to fit the bill.

"Ally," Talia says, "tell us about you."

"Well, I'm getting my master's degree in business management at UNLV." Ally shuffles some files into a drawer. "I only have ten to fifteen hours a week to work, and this seems like it would offer great experience in schedule management and client support."

"Do you have experience working with sensitive information, Ally?" Talia asks.

"I worked as a student caller during my undergrad

program, so I had access to a lot of personal information through that."

"And what about serving in a gatekeeper capacity?"

"I worked closely last semester for a professor who had me managing his scheduling. He was in the middle of a huge research project and needed close time management. I screened all requests for meetings and worked with him to prioritize, so he could optimize his work time."

"Boris, do you have any questions for Ally?" Talia shares a look with me but I'm not sure where she's going with this.

I shrug. "Not really. I am not sure how I would utilize a person such as yourself. This idea is new to me."

"What is your relationship, may I ask?" Ally asks.

Talia sits back in her chair, her eyes narrowing. "Mr. Drăghici has hired me to take over his investment strategy."

"So it's solely professional?"

"Yes," I say, just as Talia answers the same.

"Thanks," Ally says. "So, Ms. Wentworth, since Mr. Drăghici says he's not sure how this position will work in his life, I assume the genesis of it comes from you?"

"Yes," Talia answers stiffly. "I suggested that Mr. Drăghici hire someone to assist him in organization. He's got a brutal training schedule and needs someone to help him fit in other important appointments, manage his bill payment schedule, and keep him otherwise organized. Maybe more importantly, he needs someone discreet and trustworthy."

"What am I missing here?" Ally asks, looking at me.

"I am getting ripped off by my current investment agents," I tell her. Talia groans. I've let the proverbial cat out of the bag, I think. But I see no reason to hide it. Whoever we hire needs to know what this job is really about. "I have severe dyslexia and need someone to assist in reading my mail, organizing it, and instructing me on due dates and required follow-up."

"Ah," Ally says, finally shutting the file cabinet drawer and sitting in the now-empty chair. "That makes so much more sense. And it sounds like you understand what value this role could bring to your personal life."

"I am starting to see it, the more we talk about it," I admit.

"Well, since I would be working for you, I'd love to talk with you at some point about how we might work together," Ally says. "Perhaps over coffee?"

I open my mouth to answer but am not sure what to say. Is this appropriate? I have no idea of the rules of engagement here. I just answer, "Perhaps, if we decide to move you forward as a candidate, we can do that."

Talia winks at me, a smug smile on her pretty lips, and I know I answered correctly. She says, "Okay, Ally. Well, we'll talk about each candidate once we've finished interviews and get right back to you."

Ally stands and shakes both our hands, giving us a firm grip and a final statement regarding her interest in the role. She leaves and we both stand in silence for a moment.

"You liked that she organized those files," I finally say.

"I did." Talia grins. "I wanted to see if anyone was self-starter material. She definitely was. Though I didn't like the question about our relationship. It seemed inappropriate. And asking you to get coffee and talk without me in the room? What was that?"

"I think she was trying to figure things out," I suggest. "She was trying to figure out who she would really be working for."

"You, of course." Talia tilts her head at me and gives it a little shake.

"But I'm not sure you gave her that impression."

Talia pouts, sticking out her bottom lip a bit. It's very cute and I want to laugh, but I pretend a cough instead.

"I just want to make sure we get the right person for you, Boris." She's eyeing me suspiciously now.

"I know, and I appreciate it. I guess I don't really care who we hire."

"Which is exactly why I'm being such a hard-ass in these interviews."

"And I'm okay with it." I shrug it off, hoping she lets it drop.

"So while we're waiting on the third candidate, I

should tell you about my conversation with Vlad Nechaev."

"Yes, he called me after to make sure you were really acting on my behalf. Apparently, women sometimes call and pretend to be girlfriends or wives in order to try to access the finances of their clients."

"Really? People do that?"

"Yeah, I guess so. I assured him you were who you said you were."

"Well, he was weird to me." Talia sounds annoyed which I also find cute. "He's a bit of a chauvinist."

"That's probably true."

"He said he'd talk to your advisors and have them get in touch if that's what you really wanted. Honestly, though, I am weirded out by the fact I can't just call them myself, professional to professional. Aren't you weirded out by that?"

"It has always been this way."

"Did you hire these guys yourself or did someone hire them for you?"

"I have been making money playing hockey since I was very young, Talia. I was fourteen when I left home for training and started getting a stipend from the Russian Olympic committee. It was put into an investment account right away and has been managed there ever since. Even after I came to the United States, my money went to that account. Some is directed to my local checking account, but most goes to the investment accounts. I have never met the person who makes these decisions."

"It just seems crazy to me."

"It probably is, but I didn't know any different and I've never needed much to live on, so it did not occur to me to get serious about my investments until my most recent contract. Scott, my agent, actually suggested I not divert money to overseas account managers. He helped me set up local banking, so none of my new money would go to these people. This is the first time in my career I've thought maybe I needed someone else to review how I was doing."

"I'm gonna give Scott a big kiss the next time I see him. He did you a huge favor."

I don't reply.

Scott may have indeed done me a favor, but I sure don't like the idea of Talia kissing him.

Even though I know I shouldn't think this way, I can't help feeling jealous at the idea of her kissing anybody else.

*But me.*

But me? Where did that come from? Talia told me that she didn't look like a librarian or was sexy. At that moment, I didn't comment, but in my head, I disagreed firmly. I don't know what a librarian looks like, but I do know what a sexy woman looks like and Talia is that. *But how can she not know?*

My life has been full during the last week and a half, but it doesn't mean my mind stopped wandering to Talia. I had blamed that on the interview with Scarlett, and time with Pam too. Both women had implied that it wouldn't take long for a woman to want me, Boris, and not the NHL star player. And each time, my thoughts turned to Talia. Funny, quirky, and seriously sexy Talia. And now...now I don't want her lips anywhere near Scott's. Or any other man's. Like I always do, though, I file those thoughts away and focus on the task Talia has for me today. *Interviews.*

We interview two more candidates and it is obvious, when we finish, who the best candidate is. We call Ally Armstrong and ask if she's available to come back to Talia's office.

"CONGRATULATIONS, Ally, we both felt you were the best suited for this assignment. Do you have any additional questions?" Talia tells her from behind her desk, looking so fucking hot with her glasses perched on her nose, her long hair down over her shoulders, and her tight skirt hugging all the right places as she fishes around in the file drawer for something. I've spent two hours in the presence of this smart, incredibly sexy woman. I've tried to stay focused on the interviews, but I'm not sure if I have successfully masked my attraction. Especially since the mention of the kiss—

"Thank you for the opportunity to help out," Ally says brightly, interrupting my musings. "Boris, I still think we need to have that conversation to talk more about the role before I can get started. How about right now?" I look to Talia just as her office phone rings. She motions that we should go ahead without her and picks up the call.

Just a few moments later, Ally is making note of the fact I do not drink coffee as we sit down at the Starbucks on the corner. She's got long, brown hair and bright green eyes. She's striking, I suppose, but in a harsh way. Her features are sharp like her tone. Pretty much everything about her is sharp. To the point, she lacks warmth. It doesn't matter, of course. Her job is to keep me on task.

"Do you have specific food preferences?" She starts jotting notes into her phone.

"No. I'm not picky. Though I do not love onions."

"Noted," she says. "Tell me about your practice schedule."

I walk her through our pre-season schedule, including additional training and conditioning sessions. Then I mention my concussion protocol and ongoing muscle therapy.

"Ms. Wentworth was right. You do have a lot going on."

"I do, and the season is long. We are on the road for days on end so it can be hard to figure out how to fit other things in. But you need to know my appointments with Talia are critical. She's helping me out of a...situation, and it's important she gets the time she needs with me while we sort it out." I don't feel I owe Ally any more than this right now. After she's signed an NDA and a contract maybe, but not yet.

"How does your dyslexia affect your daily life?"

I breathe in and out through my nose and push my lips to one side while I think. "I function just fine.

Playing hockey does not require a lot of reading, as you can imagine, so I'm not affected much there. At home, I do have some issues with paying bills on time, and sometimes with paying the right amount. I can use someone to organize by due date and instruct on amounts, for sure."

"I can probably do you one better by setting up auto pay on most of your bills. They'll just take what they need when it's due and you won't have to do anything at all."

"That would be great. I live very simply. I would like access to some funds of course, but most of what is left after bills will be sent to my investment accounts with Talia."

"Okay, we'll get things set up. Do you have an account already with her?"

"No," I say, sounding surprised even to my own ears. "I have spoken to her so many times, but we haven't opened the account yet."

"I'll make you an appointment to set things up for your new money. If she works things out with the previous investment managers, she can add it in."

"I will take your word for that."

Ally is a taskmaster. She grills me about my life, which I realize sounds very boring as I talk about it. She says she'll set up automatic grocery delivery for my staples and asks me to make a list while we are here. She asks if I would be comfortable with her having a key to my apartment so she can meet the delivery and also manage my bills. *Do I want that? I'm a very private person, so do I want someone in my home without my knowledge?* "I'll have to think about that," I say.

As we finish, she asks, "Do you have children, a wife or girlfriend?"

I shake my head realizing it's a valid question, even though I find it annoying.

"Good," she says. "Okay, I'll work up a plan and text you tomorrow."

I nod, standing. After I pick up a cup of coffee to go for Talia, we quickly and silently walk back to the office.

Talia is peering at her computer screen as we enter but she smiles widely when I hand her the paper cup. "That is the best thing I've seen all day."

I want to tell her that her beautiful smile is the best thing I've seen all day. It nearly made my heart stop, if I'm being honest. I can't tell her though. It's inappropriate considering our working relationship.

Instead, I just nod and sit down. I witness Ally sign the NDA and contract, which will only be effective once her references have been contacted. Talia made it clear to Ally that a thorough background check would take place before any access was granted to my personal business. I could end up in the same situation I was before if I'm not cautious. Ally signs the documents and tells Talia we need to set up a time to get an investment account established so that she can work with Crush finance to assure anything above and beyond living expenses gets invested. Talia says she and I can work on getting the account established, no problem, and Ally says she would like to start by setting up regular investment meetings twice a month.

They converse as if I'm not in the room, after which Ally turns to me and promises we'll work on more personal issues in the next few days. I attempt to shake her hand but she goes in for a hug instead, wrapping her arms around me and pressing herself flush against my body. I stand stiffly as it happens, my eyes flitting to Talia, whose eyebrows are raised high on her forehead. Ally walks out. *What the hell just happened?*

As soon as she's out the door, I voice my thoughts. "Ally is...aggressive."

"You can't sleep with her."

Shocked by the comment, I turn sharply to find Talia studiously poring over something on her desk. She appears to look uninterested, but the slight crease between her eyes gives her away. *Is she angry at me?*

"I would never cross a professional line like that."

She stares up at me, eyes narrowed and dark, her pretty mouth set in a subtle frown. I have a very serious urge to take her in my arms and kiss that frown away. I know that thought is taboo though, so I take a deep breath and try to will it away. I expect her to say more on the matter but instead, her cheeks turn pink as she looks around, her eyes ultimately landing on a blank space on the wall. "I'll set up the account appointment in a week," she says finally, her eyes still directed at the wall. "I'll work through Ally to set it up. Hopefully I can get some information from your Russian investment managers by then."

I start to thank her but am thrown off when she stands abruptly, mumbling something about needing the restroom. Stepping around the corner into her tiny office bathroom, she goes in and shuts the door behind her with a bang.

Is that my cue to leave? Is she upset? Because I did what she asked and hired Ally? I signed up with her firm as a client. What the fuck did I do wrong? And even worse, why on earth does she think I would ever consider sleeping with Ally?

Frustrated, I leave her office and take a slow walk back to my apartment.

LATER, when I'm picking at my uninspiring microwaved dinner, I remember our first dinner together and Talia moaning out loud when she took a bite of her hamburger.

While playing on the Xbox, a character with white-blonde hair and black glasses appears in the game and instantly reminds me of Talia.

While watching sports highlights on TV, one of the feature stories is about a baseball player whose name I recognized on the files in Talia's office. I wonder if they have ever met, and if so, how well they know each other.

I cannot shake thoughts of Talia Wentworth from invading my head no matter what I do. She's always there, tempting me to my most private fantasies where she's at center stage.

Later, when I'm enjoying the hot spray of the shower on my skin, I'm *still* wondering what in the hell that was between us in her office earlier, and why she seemed so flustered. But since I'm all alone, I am one hundred percent free to indulge myself in a much-needed whack session while I think about her.

Of course, my thoughts on the lovely Talia only grow more focused as the hot water washes my long day away. The shape of her lips. The color of her eyes. That pale skin I'd like to taste, and that long blonde hair of hers I'd like to tug on. The way her cheeks and chest flush when she's upset. How much I'd love the chance to soothe her upset feelings away. I imagine what she looks like naked, knowing it has to be a spectacular sight, and wonder what she's like during sex. I go further and picture her with me in the shower as I take my cock in hand and give it a good stroke. The things I'd love to do to her tiny, sexy body if she were right here with me, naked, wet, and willing in my arms. I'd have her screaming my name in pleasure until we were forced out because the hot water was drained. Then I'd take great care in toweling all that creamy skin dry before carrying her to my bed and having her again until my cock stopped working. Yes, it has been a while since I've fucked. But Talia has me far more wound up than any other woman. Everything about her turns me on.

The strokes up and down my shaft become faster, a twist at the end of each pass just to help things along. My thighs and abs start to tense and tighten as the familiar sensations start from my balls, signaling that I'm about two seconds away from the blasting orgasm I desperately need right now.

It's my dirty fantasy, but it's so good imagining being inside Talia, my impossibly hard cock filling her deep as I start to come. The stuff jets out of me in a rush, joining the soap suds and water as it swirls down the drain and washes away. The good feelings stay with me though, even later when I'm in bed trying to fall asleep.

So fucking good.

But I force myself to sleep before the thoughts become more and I have to get back into the shower to do it all over again.

# 14
# tread lightly

Talia

Maybe it was a mistake to hire someone for him. At least, someone so pretty. I mean, those green eyes? They were like emeralds. Also, what if Ally takes his money and doesn't really help him? No. When I spoke to Professor Binnington, he gave her a glowing report, so I could trust in that. But college students can be so irresponsible.

No, she seems really on top of things, serious about doing a good job. It will be fine. And that hug? She was probably just trying to warm things up, right? I mean, I've hugged clients before and it didn't mean a thing.

Besides, what do I care if Ally flirts with Boris? It's none of my business. I shouldn't have said anything about him not sleeping with her. It's his business, I suppose. It will be fine. He says he wouldn't ever cross the line anyway, so there's nothing to worry about there. I just needed to find him someone to help with all his stuff. I found the person and now it's on him to figure out their working relationship, right?

My job is to assure Ally does the job she was hired for. All I have to do is try to make sure Boris is protected while he gets his finances in order—the job *I* was hired for.

*He's a client and it can't happen anyway.*

God knows I don't want more upheaval in my life.

*But he's really nice and so, so, sexy...*

No. Can't have. Cannot have the hot hockey man. He's off limits. O.F.F.

I decide to take a power walk around the block to get my head in the right place. I call my best friend, Parker, who still lives back in San Francisco.

"Hey, Tallie." She uses the nickname only she is allowed to utter.

"Hey, Parker." My voice sounds glum even to my ears.

"What's up sister?"

"Just taking a head-clearing walk. Thought I'd check in and see what's up with you."

"The dog grooming business is just booming. Been up to the armpits in dog hair and shampoo all damn day."

"Why do you work there if you hate it so much?"

"It pays the bills as you well know. Dancing is fun but there's irregularity with the paychecks."

Parker is a professional dancer with the Presidio Dance Theater in San Francisco. She works harder than anyone I've ever met, and that's saying a lot because I work pretty damned hard, myself. She dances about twenty hours a week—more when she has a show—plus takes on all the hours she can fit in at her other job. She took the gig at Shi-Shi-Shihtzu because they promised she'd be doing social media and events, and she thought that would help if she ever got to the point where she had her own company or studio. More often than not, though, they're understaffed and she ends up doing more dog grooming than she ever wanted.

"How's Sin City?" she asks. "Are you sinning a lot? Please tell me you're sinning a lot."

"Have you met me?"

"I have met you. You sexed your hot client. That's positively sinful and I'm damn impressed."

"Hot, married client," I say, groaning. "Definitely going to hell for that; and being a homewrecker is *not* something to be proud of. I've had more than my share. No more sinning necessary."

"Whatever, it's a two-way street. He could have told you about her. Or, better yet, not slept with someone other than his wife." *She's right.* I know she's absolutely right. But there is still a momentous amount of guilt because I should have used my intelligence and not listened to my raging hormones.

"I don't want to talk about him."

"Oh-kay. How's business?"

"Really good, actually. I've got a good base already, keeping me busy. I think I'll hit Howard's target of five new clients this month."

"That's good," she says through a clearly audible yawn.

"Money management is boring, I get it, but I have some fun, new clients. Angie is one of those Vegas showgirls who wear the teeny outfits and the big headdresses."

"Does Angie wear her costume into the office?"

"Ha! No. She looks very normal when she comes in. But she's making bank. Maybe I should become a showgirl."

"Talia, I hate to tell you this, but you would probably fall on your ass."

"Yes, probably true." I sigh dramatically. "I'm also working with a hockey player."

"There we go. Is he hot?"

"Irrelevant. I am just trying to help my clients toward long-term investment success. What they look like doesn't matter."

"So he's hot then?"

"He's good looking, yes."

"Single?"

"Ugh. Yes."

"Why ugh?"

"Ugh because I think Boris is a really nice guy. And he's really cute. And I think sexy thoughts about him sometimes. But I can't have him because we all know how the last client sleepover went."

"Sexy thoughts? Like what kind of sexy thoughts?"

I make a noise but don't answer.

"You've got a crush," Parker accuses.

"Do not."

"You do too, friend. And whatever. He's sexy and single. Plus his name is Boris and yours is Natalia. So close to Natasha, you're nearly the *Rocky & Bullwinkle Show* couple already. I say crush away."

"He's a client, Parker. And it's irrelevant what our names are because he doesn't find me attractive and I've sworn off relationships with clients. Boris already told me he won't cross a professional boundary anyway, so the point is moot."

"Not everyone is Mr. Cheating-Ass, Tallie."

"No, you're right. But this is a fresh start for me. I can't have Howard thinking he won't ever be able to trust me to keep my hands off the clients."

"Okay, okay, you have a point there. But tell me all about hot-hunky-hockey-Boris, anyway, because I need to know everything."

I take a deep breath in and then let it out before launching into my story about Boris. I tell my friend all about him, about his early rise to the professional ranks, his crummy Russian rip-off investment agents, and his dyslexia. I tell her I hired him an assistant to help him stay organized and then admit that I'm a little perturbed that the woman hugged him at their first meeting.

"Am I being petty?" I can't help myself from asking for reassurance. "I'm being petty, right? It was just a hug. I hug clients all the time." *No, I don't. I really, really don't.*

"You're being petty and jealous, Crushy McCrushpants."

"Totally not jealous! I just think he's really sweet and I think people have taken advantage of him. He doesn't need one more person in his life trying to get something from him."

"I guess it's possible she's a gold-digger just out to get hooked up with a rich athlete," Parker says. "But more it sounds like you don't want anyone else touching this guy if it can't be you. Maybe this guy is your guy, Tallie."

"He's not my guy."

"How do you know?"

"I just…" I groan and change the subject because I don't actually have an answer. "Are you going to come visit me soon or what?"

"Are you lonely, my little sexless love bug?"

"Yeah, kind of. I mean, I work in a tiny office by myself. I don't get much opportunity to get out and make friends."

"Aww, that's really sad. I'm sad for you."

"You don't sound sad. You sound like you're laughing at me."

"I'm not, I swear. And you're in luck because I've just decided I'm going to come on down to Sin City this weekend."

"Ask and I shall receive?"

"I was already considering it, but I can see that you need me. We'll go out dancing."

"Dancing? You have seen me dance, right? And you're sure that's the best option?"

"You'll go out dancing and you'll like it."

I laugh at this, shaking my head. "No, *you'll* go out dancing and I'll stand around and look awkward."

After we get a plan in place, I tell my best friend

just how much I love her before hanging up. I really do love her. She's honest and funny and high energy. She's way extroverted, which is the total opposite of me, of course, and she pulls me out of my comfort zone when I really need it most.

Like that time I moved to a new city all by myself.

THE NEXT DAY, whilst attempting to remove yet another food stain from my clothing—this time ketchup on my beige linen slacks—I receive my return call from none other than the Russian fixer himself, Mr. Vlad Nechaev.

"Vlad, good to hear from you."

"Do not say that just yet, little firecracker," he says in his thick accent.

"What a strange thing to say. Do you have bad news for me?"

"Are you sure you want to poke this bear?"

"What bear?" I can feel my face scrunching up in annoyance as I tap my pen on a notebook. "This is just business. We all want what's best for the client, right?"

Vlad chuckles darkly. "Yes, I suppose. Well, you can speak with Tolya Popov about Boris's accounts. Tread lightly, is my advice to you."

I snort at this. What is this, the Russian mafia? Jesus Christ. "I just want to talk to him about transferring Boris's accounts. It's not the end of the world."

He laughs into the phone by way of a response, clearly amused by me. And I don't like the sound of Vlad's laughter at all, especially when the sinister chuckling sends a shiver rolling down the length of my back. Can you say creepy as fuck with a side of revulsion?

"Don't say I did not warn you, my dear Natalia."

# 15
# a terrible wingman

Boris

Thankfully, we've moved on from the start-series drills Coach had us doing for team building. I think they've helped, though, because the guys now joke and talk with me like anyone else. I'm finally beginning to feel like I'm part of the team.

I try to think back on my time with other teams in my career and I realize that this is the first team I've played on with so many superstars. Max Terry has assembled a motley crew of ultra-talented players. They've had their issues, though. Evan was a womanizer. Georg had his demons with alcohol. Viktor had major anger issues. But they've all settled down and found support and stability. They were already playing well together and I'm the interloper. I'm the one coming in with something to prove, even though I carried my team as far as we could go in Austin. The Comets were in the process of a rebuild so it made sense to trade me for more talent they could spread out across the team, which hopefully will help them down the line for making the playoffs.

I have to keep reminding myself the Crush is a winning team, a team that's gone through its own storms in order to become what it is today. I'm a disrupter where I want nothing more than to be another weapon in an already strong arsenal. It's important to me to gain the team's trust, to learn to play with them, to play on their strengths. I just want to play and be a strong contributor.

As we shower and change from the day's grueling practice, Viktor Demoskev approaches me. He's scowling, so I'm not sure what to expect.

"Viktor."

His eyes narrow as he looks down at me. Yes, he is a big man. I'm a big man and he's several inches bigger. It's not intimidating, though he tries to make it so.

"My Scarlett has insisted I apologize to you," he says, shoving his hand out for me to shake.

"Oh, *she* insisted?" I can't resist chuckling as I take his hand in a firm grip. "Well, I accept the apology, regardless of where it came from. And I hope you know I truly meant no harm, only compliment. Sorry I upset you."

"I am a bit of an ass, she tells me. Too hot-headed. I am trying to get much better because we have a child on the way."

"You will."

"It is Friday. Several of us are headed out to get beer," Viktor answers. "Would you like to join?"

I can't help but grin. "Sure, I'm in. Thanks."

He claps me on the back and heads off to finish changing. We all head down the street to a small bar, sort of off the tourist path. Georg tells me the guys used to all go to big clubs, full of women. He laughs and shakes his head as Tyler jumps in and adds, "These bunch of old farts are all tied up over their women. How's a sexy athlete supposed to get laid hanging out with a bunch of dads?" *Please, God, tell me I was not like that at his age. An arrogant fetus...*

We all grab our beers—apart from Georg, who orders a soda—and find seats around a table. There are several televisions around, each with different sporting events playing. I nurse my single beer while the other guys down theirs with ease. No one seems to mind that I'm not keeping up, and I'm content to just sit and watch sports while Evan, Georg, and Viktor all talk about their women. I tune in, mainly because I like the idea of having what they have someday—one true love to make a life with.

Tyler, blond and rowdy, bangs his fist on the table and says, "Stop mooning over these women. What the hell happened to you fuckers?" He pretends to give himself a hand job and rolls his eyes. "You're like a bunch of old fucking men. This is no fun at all. We used to have women lined up to sit on our laps. Now we're in here drinking, like, light beer and talking about our home improvement projects."

Mikhail, also single, laughs and nearly spits out his beer.

"Well, there's the door, asshole," Georg says,

gesturing to the exit. "Get gone. You know where to go if you need to get your rocks off."

I sense that this is all normal for this group. Viktor, by all accounts Tyler's best friend, grins and smacks his buddy on the back of the head. "Don't come out with us if you are going to complain the whole time."

"I'm just saying, can a brother get a break every once in a while? One night out to pick up a hot chick in a short skirt?"

Mikhail, generally pretty quiet, says, "I'm with you. Let's leave these old men and make some noise."

"Fuck yeah!" Tyler hoots. He points in Viktor's face. "You're being replaced as wingman."

"I was terrible wingman to begin with."

"That's a fuckin' truth if ever I heard one."

They bump fists before Tyler and Mikhail start toward the door. Tyler stops, though, and turns to me. "You got an old lady?"

"No." I shake my head.

"Then you're with us. Don't take this the wrong way, but you're eye candy. Chicks will talk to us because of you."

This makes me laugh. I start to say no. I should stay and hang out with the power players, right? Still, it might be fun to go out for once.

I stand and the guys give me fist bumps before telling me not to do anything they wouldn't do. I am not sure how far that goes, but I'm positive they have no clue just how boring a guy I am. I don't think I could match them, even now they are all in solid relationships.

We get a ride service that takes us up to the Strip and I realize I've never really gone out and explored the single most iconic section of Las Vegas before, even though I've been in town for weeks now. The lights and people are overwhelming in comparison to laid-back Austin. Tyler picks out a nightclub for us to try but when we head inside, it's fairly empty for a Friday night.

"It's still kind of early." Tyler checks his phone as he picks a booth near the bar. "We'll get some food. People will start coming soon."

We order and then eat, and Tyler's prediction becomes a reality. I think it's safe to say he's done this a time or two...or ten. An hour later, and a crowd has filled the place. The music starts thumping and the lights are turned down. A couple of women make a beeline for our table, asking if we have a light for their cigarettes. Tyler shakes his head and they walk away.

"Not interested?" I ask.

"Smokers? Nah."

I nod and take a sip of the beer I ordered with dinner.

"What's your type?" he asks.

I shrug.

"Wow. You're killing me with charisma, dude."

"This is not really my scene. I don't go out often."

"Surely you stepped out after games in Austin? Got your noodle wet?"

"Well yeah, of course, sometimes, but one-night-stands aren't really—"

Tyler and Mikhail's laughter cuts me off. I must look confused because they just laugh harder. Mikhail says, "Brother, this is Las Vegas. Easy sex is part of the perks."

"Have you even had sex?" Tyler asks. "You're not some forty-year-old virgin are you?"

My brows furrow. "I am not forty."

"You know what I mean. You've been laid, right?"

"Of course. But I am picky."

"Picky is one thing," Tyler says. "Picky I can deal with. You have a pair of balls and a working pecker, right?"

"Yeeees?" *Where is he going with this?*

"Good. Then it's time you got christened. Welcome to Sin City."

He stands and both Mikhail and I follow him toward the dance floor. We stand at the edge, Tyler making eyes at nearly every pretty girl in the place.

"How about her?" he asks, pointing to a buxom woman with curly hair. "Her tits are about to pop out of that dress. She's looking for a hookup."

I shake my head. "Not my style."

He keeps doing this, pointing out women he assumes are up for an easy pickup. I keep responding the same way, with total disinterest, until he finally shrugs and heads out on the dance floor with Mikhail and two young women looking to party. I stand at the railing, watching the crowd and nursing the same beer I started with. I wonder how many minutes I should stand here before I can go because I probably look creepy as fuck hanging out, staring into the crowd. I shouldn't have ever come with them tonight. This totally isn't my thing.

I head to the upper deck, hopefully where I won't look so awkward. There are several people up there, some already hot and heavy in the booths along the wall. I stand along the edge, watching the crowd below, when a blonde captures my attention.

I think that's—could it be Talia? Damn. Yes, she's totally Talia Wentworth.

She stands at the edge of the dance floor, much like I did just moments ago. In skinny, leather pants and a sleeveless, flowy top showing off her creamy skin, she looks really hot. *Exactly my type if anyone's asking.*

Her thick glasses rest on her face, which is probably the only reason I recognize her, because she isn't in her stiff work-wear. Her hair flows long and wavy around her shoulders, bright in the flashing club lights.

Wow, Talia is incredibly gorgeous tonight. I don't like the thought of feeling attracted to someone I need to have a professional relationship with, but I can't help it. And I can't look away.

She stands alone, gripping a beer bottle and swaying to the music as she watches someone on the dance floor. I follow her gaze to see a young woman gyrating against some random guy, trying to wave her out to the floor to join them. Talia just laughs and shakes her head.

I watch her for the length of two songs, trying to decide if I should go down and talk to her. I mean, this is a club. It's outside the boundary of our professional relationship. She's probably out to have a good time or hook up or whatever. Another song and at least two guys try to talk to her. Her posture is awkward, and I can tell she's either embarrassed or shy or not interested. Both guys walk away empty-handed, a fact which makes me irrationally happy.

Since I've now been staring at her for four songs, I decide I should just go down and say hello, rather than looking like a serial killer up in the balcony. I head back down the stairs, running into Tyler at the edge of the dance floor near where I last saw him. He's got a woman on each arm and Mikhail trails closely behind with another.

"One for each of us," Tyler says proudly.

My gaze is still focused on Talia across the room. Tyler's eyes narrow and he nods. "Okay. More for me, then. Quit being a fuckin' creeper and go talk to her."

Tyler's got a point.

So as their little group wanders off to do whatever they can get away with in a public club, I decide to take the long walk over to talk to my sexy obsession.

# 16
# girls who wear glasses

Talia

This is a disaster. I feel stupid, all dressed up in Parker's slutty clothes.

I've never been a good dancer. My limbs always felt too long, too out of control. I never learned to move my body the right way and besides, this house music is crazy. People who *can* dance look stupid out there, so I know I would just up the idiot-quotient by a gajillion points.

Also, I've been hit on three times and all three guys made opening comments about girls who wear glasses. Ugh. Get original, dudes.

Parker comes off the dance floor with a huge smile on her face. She's a natural beauty, tall and lithe. As an actual dancer, she puts everyone to shame on the dance floor, but her beauty doesn't hurt either. She's got sleek, dark blonde hair, high cheekbones, perfect lips.

"You're all cute over here, looking like a total hottie, and I've seen you turn away three decent-looking dudes. How are you supposed to meet anyone if you refuse to talk to people?"

"I feel like an imposter," I say with a shrug. "Plus, all those dudes used basically the same line on me."

"Girls who wear glasses?"

"Ugh, yes."

"Lame. Well, the guy I was dancing with was totally hot. I guess he does sound and stuff? for the big acts who come in for concerts."

"Sounds like an interesting job." I try to sound engaged but I couldn't care less to be honest.

"I mean, it's hard to talk with the music blaring. He could really move." Parker fans herself and looks around, a big smile on her face.

"Well, you should go find him, then. Talk to him, Parker."

"What about you?"

"I'd rather just go home and order a pizza."

"What a party pooper."

"But when have you ever known me to be otherwise?"

"Well," she says, a sly grin on her face, "you can go if you want, but there's a big, hot-looking dude over there who's been eyeballing you for quite some time. I think he might be disappointed to see you leave."

I look and my heart does a little bounce inside my chest. It's Boris. I catch his eye but he looks down. If the lighting was better, I'd swear he was blushing.

Still, I'm really glad to see a familiar face. "That's my hockey client!"

"Well no wonder you're crushing on your puck-money dude. Holy hell, he's the freaking poster boy for hot athletes."

I laugh at her name for Boris. "That's hilarious, Parker. Puck-money dude. I guess it's a pretty accurate descriptor though. Should I go say hi to him?"

"Yes, yes, you should." Her tone is salacious. "I'm gonna go find my hot dancing hunk, too. Text me if you leave."

"What about you?"

"I'll do the same."

She gives me a hug before slinking off toward the bar. Me? I put one foot in front of the other and take the few steps over to Boris because I'm fatalistic like that and gravitate toward awkward situations like the nerd I was born. At this point in my life I've just given up and owned it. I'm never going to be any different.

"Hey." *Yes, you just sounded as painfully embarrassed as you're thinking you did.*

"Hey, yourself. I saw you earlier." Smooth as silk. No awkwardness at all coming off of him. How? How does he do it?

"Earlier?"

"I mean, I thought I might talk to you earlier." He clears his throat and rubs his hand over his stubbled chin. Which, by the way, yum.

"Why didn't you?"

"I was upstairs, and you were downstairs."

"Well, I suppose that would make it hard to talk."

A silence settles between us as I mull over the fact Boris must have been watching me from the balcony.

"I also did not want it to seem weird," he blurts

unexpectedly. "I'm your client and you're out on your free time."

"It's not like you planned to talk business, though, right?"

"I suppose not." He shrugs a shoulder and takes a sip of his beer.

"So, you did plan to talk business?"

"No." Only the music fills the space between us for another minute. "I saw you kick a few guys to the curb."

So he was watching me for quite some time. Interesting. Does that mean he was too nervous to come over to say hi? I shouldn't overanalyze it, right?

"I was...they weren't my type, I guess? I mean, I wasn't interested."

"Did they ask you to dance?"

"They, um, used bad pickup lines. I didn't let them get far enough to ask me to dance. Also, I mean, I'm not really a very good dancer anyway, so..."

"That doesn't matter. If you'd like, we could..."

"I don't really know how," I say, giving what I think is an apologetic look. "I'll look like an idiot."

"Everyone looks stupid when they dance." Boris gives me a cute, dimpled, lopsided grin. "I'm big. I can shield you from view." He holds out a hand. "Come on, dance with me."

"I can't promise I won't step on your toes or embarrass you."

"I am not easily embarrassed, Talia."

I look up and am struck by the stark gorgeousness of a hard-stubbled jawline, and the soft lips, and the liquid brown eyes that look exactly like melted chocolate. It does beg the question... Where are the hordes of women who *I know would love to be hanging from his muscular frame right now*? In this club—where hookups are negotiated (or occurring) every minute of every hour this place is open for business. Did he send them away because he's into men instead? If so, he's probably in the wrong club tonight. But I've never felt that vibe from Boris even slightly, so if he is gay, I'm way off base. Anyway, I might never get the chance to dance with a guy this beautiful ever again. And besides all the hotness he has going on, he's also sweet. A gentleman. This will be nice. Or, as nice as me dancing will ever get, I suppose.

"Okay." I still feel reluctant, but I put my hand into his anyway, allowing him to lead me out onto the dance floor.

We find a spot along the wall and, as promised, Boris stands with his back to the crowd, acting as a shield to give me an illusion of privacy. I start to move, trying to loosen up and get my limbs under control. Boris can keep a beat. I suppose all that skating is often like a dance of sorts, so I'm not surprised he can move. He gives me that little lopsided grin of his and a thumbs-up.

I lift my shoulders and cringe.

"Just close your eyes and feel the beat," he says over the music.

I take a deep breath in through my nose and give a short nod. Closing my eyes, it takes a minute to get past the worry that people might be looking at me.

Eventually, though, I catch the beat, my body moving. I just let go, then, lost in the sound. I dip and sway, and when I open my eyes, Boris is staring at me, his eyes dark and intense. Holy ever—loving hell, he is sex on legs. Does he even know?

I feel emboldened by the expression on his face, for some reason, so I drape an arm over one of his shoulders. Suddenly, our bodies are moving together, his hand on my hip. His knee is between my legs as we move, and I can't stop thinking about how I wish it was his hand between my legs. Our eyes are locked and there is an odd energy connecting us, moving us. *I've never felt so...sensual before.* In tune. *Alive.*

We stay like that for what seems like forever, my free hand moving to his solid chest. The man feels like a stone sculpture. Christ. What must all those muscles look like under that white, button-down shirt?

My heart beats frantically in my chest. I'm sweating and thirsty, but I just want to keep touching this man.

Still, he's a client and I made a rule. This needs to stop.

As the song ends, I back away. "I'm hungry," I announce. "And thirsty."

Boris backs off, nodding. He looks away and I think he's blushing again. "Do you want to get a bite?"

"Let me tell my friend. I'll meet you outside?"

Boris nods again and shoves his hands in his pockets. I'm pretty sure he stands right there where I left him, watching me walk away, but I'm too scared to turn around and find out.

# 17

# to cross or not to cross?

Boris

The fresh air outside of the club is a relief and I grab onto the opportunity to get myself under control. Dancing with Talia was very hot. Hot enough to make my cock wake up and start demanding attention. If we'd kept going, I would've been totally hard which would have been horrifying. *And if she'd leaned in any closer, she would have felt it. Felt what she does to me.*

Now I just feel nervous. Did she realize I was so turned-on by her? Is that why she stopped so abruptly? Maybe her announcement she was hungry was just a reason to get rid of me. It seemed like she was as into the dancing as I was, as into me as I was into her. Still, we both know this is a line we shouldn't cross.

It was impossible not to focus on our bodies together. Her breasts rubbing against my chest, my leg between her legs, my hand on her hip, her hand on my chest.

Shake it off. *Shake it off, fucker.*

I wait five minutes and she doesn't come. Was I a creep? Was it too forward to ask her to dance?

Another five minutes and I'm positive she's ditched me. I deserve it, of course. I crossed a line with her. Shit. Now I'll have to face her at her office. I'll have to begin with an apology. And be prepared to grovel because I need her help with my fucked-up financials. I don't want to lose her expertise. I should've just left her alone to her evening. She just looked so incredibly sexy and gorgeous standing—

"Hey," a voice says to my right.

I turn and there she is, all white-blonde hair and creamy skin. Her cheeks are pink, flushed. My mind immediately goes to inappropriate wondering where else she might be blushing.

"There you are," I say, my voice more hoarse than usual. Maybe she'll think it's from the smoke in the club and not because I'm thinking filthy thoughts about her. I clear my throat and ask, "What kind of food are you in the mood for?"

"Would pizza be okay?"

"Perfect choice."

We start walking, neither of us really sure where the nearest pizza place might be. Talia pulls out her phone and does a map search, and we follow the little dot until we find a greasy-looking pizza shop.

At the counter, Talia orders a small pepperoni pizza and a large soda and then turns to me and says, "What are you having?"

A barking laugh escapes my throat, which makes

Talia grin broadly. She looks young, sweet. I want to kiss her so badly.

*Pizza, right. Order some fucking pizza, creep! Get your head back on your shoulders.*

I manage to order my own pizza and another beer (my third of the night) and pay, pleased that she's let me this time. She fills her soda cup at the machine before grabbing seats at a high-top table.

"Can you really put down a whole pizza by yourself?" I ask, curious. "Never mind. I saw you eat that hamburger as big as your head. I know the answer already."

She smiles prettily up at me but stays quiet.

"So, what was it like to go to college so young?" I ask, genuinely curious. She's done a great deal for someone so young.

"It was fine. I mean, I was always really focused. I spent a lot of time studying and did a few extracurriculars. I lived in the dorms the entire four years, so I never had that off-campus experience."

"Not a lot of partying for you?"

"Not really," she answers. "I wasn't old enough to drink for most of it and I was terrified I'd get in trouble. I got shit-faced a few times, but nothing to write home about."

"No boyfriends?"

"A few, but nothing serious."

"Do you have a boyfriend now?"

Talia's responding grin is flirtatious. "Nope."

"That's good," I say as our eyes meet. There's a bit of a nervous flop in my stomach jarring me back to reality. I look away and ask her another question instead. "Is pizza your favorite food?"

"All food is my favorite food," she says. "Pizza ranks pretty high, though. You?"

"I like it a lot, too."

"Well, we have that in common, then."

"I was worried you were not going to come out of the club earlier," I admit. "I thought maybe I'd gone too far. That I'd crossed a line." *Please say no. Please tell me I didn't.*

"I was the one humping your leg. I'm pretty sure I should be apologizing to you."

I try to hide the grin threatening to split my face. Talia Wentworth is so interesting to me. Awkward and shy, yet such a mouth on her. She's so direct sometimes. It's refreshing and frightening at the same time.

"I didn't mind at all. I liked it. Probably too much."

Talia bites her lip then turns away, hiding her face with her hair. When she turns back to me, the subject changes. "So, how are things with Ally?"

"We haven't had time to meet yet."

"Boris, what the hell? How are you supposed to get organized if you don't utilize the person you hired to help you get organized?" Talia is even more beautiful when she's annoyed.

"Well, I'm not used to the idea of having an assistant. But I promise you, I'll call her tomorrow and find time, though."

"You'd better," Talia says, pointing her finger at

me. "If you want me to manage her tasks, I can do that."

"No, you've done enough. More than is probably normal. Thank you. I promise to call."

Thankfully the pizza arrives and interrupts the Ally conversation.

*Thank God.* Because I can't tell Talia that despite feeling nothing but uncomfortable when Ally hugged me, I felt desperate for more of Talia in that club. As if I was starving for her touch. Starving for time with her.

And now I get to watch Talia eat, which is entertainment in and of itself as she takes big bites of pizza and goes to town on her small pepperoni. I'm utterly fascinated. Because the pizza is sizzling hot—to which she appears oblivious as she shovels bites in. Also, where does all that food go? She's thin—her body is perfect, from what I can tell. I just don't know where the calories go.

After eating two slices in the time it takes mine to cool to a reasonable temperature, Talia takes a long drink of her soda. She covers her mouth and burps into her hand, audible enough that I can clearly hear it.

"Sorry, my bad." She giggles and blushes at the same time.

"That was kind of epic though. Almost as good as one of my hockey teammates could do."

"I feel very accomplished, then," she answers, grinning sexily.

I'm transfixed.

Also fucked…

THE NIGHT AIR IS CRISP, and the brief break in temperature is appreciated as we walk. I insisted on walking Talia home, since it's now very late, and the people still out and about on the sidewalks are probably very drunk.

"I forgot to tell you, I tried calling your investment guys in Russia," she says.

"Oh?"

"Yeah, some guy named Tolya? Vlad was his usual weird and cryptic self when he called to give me his name and number. Then when I got this Tolya guy on the line, he told me to keep my nose where it belongs. I'm pretty sure he was really telling me to fuck off in so many words."

"What? Are you sure?"

"Yeah. There was some Russian interlaced into the context of his short conversation with me that definitely didn't sound like pleasantries so, connecting the dots…" she trails off with a wave of her hand in my direction.

I cringe inwardly at the thought of Talia being insulted by Tolya, even if she didn't understand his use of Russian words. Fucker is on my shit list now. "I'll be calling him tomorrow to say I want my accounts moved immediately. That is unacceptable behavior on his part, and he owes you an apology to make this right."

Talia brightens at this. "Oh, I don't care about that asshole. I'm just happy for you. This is very exciting, Boris, you won't regret it."

"I know I won't."

We talk a little about her strategy for building my investments back up. There are some decisions for me to make, but I mostly defer to her judgment because I know she knows what she's doing. She chatters on and on until finally saying, "This is me."

I look up and realize we're at my apartment building. I can't help laughing.

"What's so funny?"

"I live here, too."

"No way."

I nod, my lips in a tight smile, eyebrows raised.

"Prove it." Talia puts her hands on her hips and tilts her head at me in a challenge. "There's no way we've lived in the same apartment building and not known it all this time."

"I filled out the forms for my new accounts," I tell her, chuckling. "You didn't recognize the address?"

"Give me a break. I just moved here. I barely know my own address yet," she laughs, still shaking her head in disbelief.

We walk inside, saying hello to Jimmy, one of the doormen for the building, and take the elevator to the eighth floor. I walk her to my door, pull out my key and make a big show of unlocking the door.

"No frigging way," she says, stepping inside. "What a funny coincidence. And why is your apartment so much bigger than mine?"

I show her around my tidy space. It's pretty sparsely decorated, with mostly hockey memorabilia on the shelves. I have a living room with a large, comfortable couch and a flat-screen television on one wall, my game systems stashed on a shelving unit below. My kitchen has an eat-in island, and then there's my bedroom, with a king-sized bed and dresser, a large attached master bathroom decked out in marble. It should feel strange having someone here, reminding me how often I am alone. Yet, this is Talia. I want her in this space, to enjoy the spa bath in the bathroom, to eat a huge meal in the kitchen...to sleep in my bed.

"This place is huge," Talia marvels. "Seriously."

"It's not really that big," I say, looking around. "Smaller than my place in Austin, actually. But it's fine. It's just me so I don't need a lot."

"It's a total dude space, though. Like, you need someone to come in and make this feel more like home," Talia says with a cute nod.

"I have moved a lot in my life, so I tend to pack light. Maybe someday, if I settle down or have a wife or whatever."

Our eyes meet and Talia's face settles into a weird expression that I find very hard to read. Have I made her upset I wonder?

"What about your place? It can't be much smaller?"

"Follow me," she answers.

We walk back out into the hallway and I lock the door quickly before stepping back onto the elevator with her. At the fifth floor, we get back out and head to her door. She opens it and steps aside, her arm out wide. "Voila! Home sweet home."

First, I'm totally overwhelmed. There are books and pictures and papers all over. Tall shelves lined with books. A yoga mat and exercise ball in one corner. It's just the one room, that I can surmise, plus a small bathroom and kitchenette with a counter and two tall high-backed stools. The only other big furniture items besides the bookshelves is a massive blue velvet chaise with a soft-looking blanket thrown messily over a stack of books at one end. There's no television, only a laptop charging on the floor, haphazard like the rest of the place. There's also a floor lamp and a big basket with what looks like a lot of yarn balls inside it.

"This is you?" I ask.

"This is me."

"It's kind of—" I clear my throat. "It's messy. Like your office."

"Hey!" She play-punches me in the arm. "I have my own unique organization system. You want something to drink?"

"I could use some water. Thanks."

Talia steps into the kitchenette and announces that she needs some tea. As she embarks on the effort to make it, I look more closely at the rows and rows of books. I run my fingertips over the spines, thinking I should probably go.

But I don't want to. *It feels like a home, yet she's only been here for a short time. Maybe it's just her.*

I realize this whole place smells like Talia. A mixture of coffee and cake and something slightly fruity. It's an utterly intoxicating smell that I want to breathe in for just a little while longer.

I'm into some deep trouble now with Talia Wentworth. I know it. I wonder if she knows it, too. There's no use trying to deny what I'm feeling every time I'm around her.

I like her. A lot. If only touching her wasn't taboo. If only kissing her wasn't forbidden.

*If only she could be mine.*

# 18
# read to me

Talia

"Have you read any of those?" I ask when I realize Boris is touching my most prized possessions on this earth. Other than LuLu, of course. But LuLu is not really a possession. She's my beloved fur-child, rescued from a dirty alley in San Francisco when I stepped back there to empty the office trash into the bin. This filthy little ball of fluff came flying out from behind the bin when the trash lid banged closed and scared her. Obviously starving, she came right up to me when I returned a few minutes later with a can of cat food purchased from the market around the corner. Thank goodness for pop-top lids. I opened the can, set it down at my feet, and fell into instalove with the little street urchin while watching her devour her first real food in lord knows how long. I fed her for three days before I caved and brought her home with me. I gave her a bath in my kitchen sink the first night. I discovered her fur was pure white once all the filth was washed away, and that she was a female. Poor baby was very underweight from living on the streets, but otherwise healthy. The vet told me it was a miracle she wasn't pregnant when I found her. He estimated her age to be less than a year old, around six to nine months or so. The two of us never looked back. LuLu was my cat and I was her mother from that day forward. And she is also currently hiding from the very handsome Russian in her home.

It would normally bother me what Boris is doing right now. I don't like people touching my books. Like seriously, that's a thing with me. Still, he's looking at them with something akin to awe, so it softens my inclination to be protective of my prized collection of tomes.

"What do you think?" I don't miss the heavy sarcasm in his tone.

Right. His dyslexia must make it hard to get through a novel. I mean, heck, he can't get through a contract or an electric bill. It makes me sad for him, though I try not to let it show in my face. I wouldn't want people pitying me if I were in his position.

"I don't know what I'd do without books in my life," I reply from the kitchen where I'm busy filling a cup with ice and filtered water for him and putting the kettle on for my tea. When I return to the main space and hand Boris his glass, he's totally focused on me, studying me intently as he thanks me for the water.

"You look sad," he says softly.

"I do? I'm sorry." No use denying it. He's caught me fair and square.

"Please don't be sad for me. I have dyslexia, but otherwise my life is pretty sweet." He gifts me with one of his perfected half-smiles; just a small quirk of his pretty lips that contain the power to melt me into a puddle of goo instantaneously.

"I know that," I blurt out, hoping to smooth over my gaffe. "God, I do know. You're an Olympic athlete, for crying out loud. You're an eight-figure superstar playing at the very top ranks of the NHL. I'd say that's more than sweet, Boris. It's pretty freaking rare and amazing. Still, I just really love to read. I love immersing myself into other worlds. It brings me peace, you know? My mind just goes and goes most of the time, and reading helps me control all the random and crazy flitting through my head on any given day. I can't imagine not having it in my life."

Boris sips his water and continues his examination of my very-crowded bookshelves. I take the moment to surreptitiously admire his backside, then give myself a mental smack-down for it. *You can't do this with him, fool! You shouldn't have been dry-humping him at the club either, but here we are...*

"There are so many here," he comments in his light accent. It's probably a mixture of Czech and Russian with some American thrown in. I can tell he's lived a lot of places and been around a lot of different people.

"Well, I read a lot." I feel kind of embarrassed

explaining my life but somehow it doesn't bother me explaining to Boris. "I'm a bit of an introvert. I'd rather hang with fictional people than real people most of the time."

"Oh," he says, straightening to his full height and turning toward me. "I can go if you—"

"No!" I put up my hands, then laugh at the way I just yelled at him. I swear I have no social skills. "I didn't mean it like that. Not that you should go or whatever. I just—"

"It's okay, Talia. I get it. I like my alone time, too. I'm not much for partying like the place we were at tonight. I just went along with a few of the guys since they invited me to join them, and because we're still building our team cohesion. Remember I told you about it?"

"I remember." I nod in agreement before blurting, "You should know I don't go out clubbing either. My best friend Parker came in from San Francisco and she made me go. She put me in these clothes." I flop my hands helplessly to indicate the super sexy outfit she forced me to wear. "I would have chosen something a lot less...slutty."

"No. Not at all. You look lovely tonight, but I'm sure you would have looked just as stunning in anything else you chose to wear."

I feel my cheeks flush with heat at his compliment. I'm not used to attention and compliments from men, and certainly not from men who look like him. He's downright dangerous when he's throwing out phrases like "you look lovely tonight" in my direction. Jesus.

Boris turns back to the books and asks, "Which one is your favorite?"

"Ha! That's like asking which kid is someone's favorite. There's no way to choose just one. I have a long list of favorites. I love classics and fantasy and young adult and romance and contemporary and poetry—"

"Okay, okay, I get it," Boris says, cutting me off with a laugh. He grabs a random book from the shelf and hands it over. "Read to me?"

Is he for real? He wants me to read to him right now.

I'm about to protest or make a dumb joke or something when the tea kettle screams. This gives me a minute to process his request. I turn off the burner, remove the outer wrapper from my teabag, and put everything into a mug, spending too much time fussing with the sugar and the milk probably. But the whole time, I'm going over this strange request in my head. Yes, Boris is my client. Furthermore, it would be kind of strange to do story time with a client. Wouldn't it? But then if I'm being totally honest, there is something brewing between us, or we'd never have done all that sexy grinding together on the dance floor.

We wouldn't be here together right now. *And I wouldn't know what the touch of his hands on my skin would feel like either.*

And then there's the part where I feel bad for him.

He doesn't know the magic of books because his disability has kept him from experiencing it. That, more than anything, makes me comfortable with this whole deal. I can read him part of a book, even a whole book, because it might be a life changing realization for him to discover the awesomeness of the literary world.

Finally, I take a deep breath and turn, my steaming cup of tea in hand. But Boris is right there. And I'm me so…my hot cup of tea spills. This time not on me, but on Boris's nice white shirt.

He yelps—because, you know, it's freaking hot—and immediately pulls his shirt up over his head. "I'm sorry! I'm sorry!" I yell, dashing for the kitchen, grabbing a dishcloth and running it under cool water. Racing back over, I reach out and dab the cool cloth onto his chest and abs where the hot tea made contact. It takes a second or two for me to realize I'm touching the bare skin of his well-defined chest and abs.

I back away, the cloth still in my hand, my hand still halfway between him and me, and apologize again, feeling helpless. "Shit. I'm such a klutz. I am so damn sorry for hurting you."

Boris takes the hand with the cloth in it and catches my gaze. I look away, licking my lips. But looking away from the intensity in his eyes means taking in the rest of him. Powerful shoulders, washboard abs, bulging biceps. There's a patch of dark hair on his chest, a thin happy trail that leads down underneath his jeans. And that big, beautiful dragon tattoo snaking up one arm. He looks sexy and fit, with just the right amount of naughty and nice.

Christ. I might pass out. This guy is...he can't be real.

"It's okay," he says quietly. "Accidents happen and I shouldn't have startled you like that."

I gulp, giving him a weak nod in response. He lets go my hand and returns the dishcloth to me.

"Well, now I have to read you that book, I suppose." I make a half-hearted attempt at a joke.

"Thank you." That's all he says before we wander over to the chaise. I sit in my favorite spot, my feet curled under me as I pull my favorite chenille blanket up over my lap. This is a cue for LuLu, who's been hiding who-knows-where, to jump up on my lap with a loud greeting.

"Hello, my sweet girl." I focus all my attention on petting her fluffy, white fur. She purrs and rubs on me, happy to have me at home.

"Who is this?" Boris asks.

"This is LuLu, my spoiled fur-child."

He reaches over to offer his hand for her to sniff. "Hello LuLu. You are as beautiful as your mother."

Captivated yet again by another one of his compliments, I feel myself blushing. "You're quite good for our ego, sir. Maybe we'll invite you over more often."

"I only speak the truth, Talia," he says with a serious look on his handsome face.

*My God, how can he look at me like that?*

I glance down at the book. Iain Cooper's, *Leaving*

*Area 51*. It's a sci-fi with a strong female lead and a heavy dose of romance. It was good. Not one of my top ten, but I can see a dude liking it.

As I start to read, Boris leans back into the chaise beside me and closes his eyes. I might worry he's fallen asleep, but I see his face reacting as I read. His lips are a distraction as they twitch in response to funnier lines in the book. I want to kiss those lips more than I'd like to admit.

I read about three chapters before a big yawn interrupts me. Boris opens his eyes and studies me.

"You're tired."

"It's way past my bedtime."

"One more chapter and then I'll go?"

I can't say no to him. I cannot. And I certainly don't want to, either. And then there is the fact that he's still half-naked. So, I swallow my lust and turn the page.

I start the next chapter, but this time he doesn't close his eyes. He watches me the whole time. Every word. That dark look returns to his eyes—the one I saw when we were dancing at the club together.

Is he...turned on? By my reading?

I finish the chapter and then mark the page. We stare at each other for a long time and my breathing feels labored. I can't deny it. I am very, very attracted to this man. He seems...just so good. A good guy. It's so much more than him having a handsome face and a chiseled body. It's *Boris,* the man. It's all of him. I like everything about him, and now at least I should start by being honest, and by admitting that *I want him.*

He's still a client, though. I made myself a promise I wouldn't cross the line ever again.

I stand abruptly, LuLu flying off the chaise with an annoyed meow. The blanket falls to the floor as I grab for it, stammering something about needing to check my phone to see if Parker has messaged me.

He's right there, on his feet, so close to me. His big body fills up the space between us, and suddenly, it's hard to breathe. But now I know it's not just me, because I can see the bulge in his jeans. He's hard. Words come out of his mouth in that raspy, ultra-sexy, Boris-speak he does so well. I have no idea what he just said, because I can't tear my eyes away from his huge cock pushing against denim fabric.

There you have it. I'm weak.

And so very turned on by the sexy-Boris show that I'm no longer a rational woman trying to do the right thing.

Everything aches. My nipples are hard, straining against the lace of my bra. I'm wet, aching, and hot between my legs. And then I notice his nipples are hard, too, and I can't help it. Goddamn, I can't help it. I reach out and touch him. I touch his bare chest with my palm before running a fingertip over his nipple.

He shivers, a soft moan coming from somewhere deep in his throat. His face is intense, his eyes so, so dark and hungry.

I pull away, biting one side of my bottom lip. "I'm sorry," I whisper. "I shouldn't have crossed that line."

"I'm going to kiss you now, Talia."

I barely make out his words, he said them so quietly. But still, he's warning me for what's about to happen. It's now on me to put a stop to this.

I can't.

I won't...

He leans down closer...closer...

And then his lips are touching mine and his hand is snaking into my hair to cradle my head. His other hand is on my lower back pulling me firmly against him as he takes full control of the kiss.

And I'm hopelessly and utterly lost to him. Whatever he's going to do I am fully on board. *Yes, please, yes.*

It's not a hard kiss, but it's not gentle either. It's perfect as Boris works on giving me a kiss I'll never forget for as long as I live. His lips move over mine as if he's trying to devour me. He flicks his tongue against my bottom lip, demanding more. I open to him as his tongue licks against mine, ravishing my mouth with masterful control. He kisses me in a way that leaves me reeling with only one thought in mind.

*I need so much more of this.*

He kisses me like he owns me. Tasting me over and over and over until I'm dizzy with desire, melting into his hard body, letting him hold me up. And he definitely is holding me up, for now.

Maybe he can read my mind because he presses me back down onto the chaise and crawls on top of me. Not crushing me but caging me in underneath him. I feel so small beneath his big body, but it feels perfect and right because we fit together like puzzle pieces waiting to be snapped in place. The hard length of his cock rocking into me is making me so wet for him. I sigh when he nudges my legs apart with his knees and sinks deeper against me, his hips rocking his hard cock over my sensitive clit in tandem with what his tongue is doing in my mouth. A steady rhythm of sexy that will give me a fantastic orgasm if he keeps doing it and doesn't stop.

*Oh God, I will die if he stops.*

It's ecstasy being held and kissed and caressed by someone who knows what he's doing. He takes my bottom lip in his teeth and gives me a gentle bite. He does it over and over—his teeth coming together to snag my lip in a tenuous hold before dragging away until it pops free again. I'm delirious, and utterly past trying to keep control, to keeping this sweet and light between us.

It's no longer sweet when I take his hand and guide it down the front of the thin leather leggings I wore tonight.

It's no longer light when he fingers my pussy and feels how wet he's made me.

It's downright dirty and delicious when I slide my hand inside the front of his jeans to find his cock pulsing hot and hard, wrap my fingers around the silky skin, and stroke him up and down. He growls into my mouth and rasps out some Russian words. I have no idea what he just said but my active imagination is extremely good at visualizing. It sounded animalistic, like a man telling me what he'd like for us to do.

*I want to fuck you.*

Yes, yes, yes...

And then Boris does the one thing that will most certainly cause my imminent death.

*I will die now.*

Because he just stopped.

# 19
# you sick or something?

Boris

I break off the kiss so suddenly it feels painful when I move myself off her with a frustrated groan. *Because I don't do this.* I don't do casual sex. Honestly, this didn't feel casual with Talia, but I know we've both been drinking tonight. Still, it's way over the line, and we have to continue to work together. Make that, I *want* to continue working with her. I can't have some decision I made irrationally in the heat of the moment get in the way of what we're trying to accomplish together.

As I back away, Talia looks crestfallen, confused, and upset. She's frowning and biting her bottom lip again. Her stormy blue eyes are staring up at me with a whole lot of "what the fuck" swirling around in their depths. It's just fucking awful.

"I'm so sorry, Talia. I apologize to you for that—whatever that was. It's just that we—we can't do this. You're beautiful and kind and I really like you very much, but we have a professional relationship. I don't want to make it weird by crossing the line. Well, by crossing the line further than I just did. Again, I'm sorry. Please say you understand?"

She nods, but she's still biting her lip and I can see that her eyes are now watery. Have I made her cry? God, what fucking asshole I've been to her. Why did I allow things between us get so extremely out of control?

"I'm really sorry." I know I'm babbling as I head for the door, grabbing my shirt from the counter as I pull her door open. I can't help from looking back at her one more time. Talia stands in the same place where I left her, looking so beautiful, and rejected, and not happy with me at all.

*I hate this. It's fucked-up and I caused it.*

I want to rush back over to her and take her in my arms and kiss the ugliness of the last few moments away until she's humming with desire again. *Because that was one of the hottest moments of my life. Because tasting her, feeling her...God, I want that so much.* But that would just make everything even worse between us, so I walk out her door instead, shutting it behind me with a heavy click.

As I step onto the lift to go to my floor, Talia's friend from the club gets out. She nods at my bare chest and grins, pointing with her eyes to Talia's door.

I hear her go inside and say, "Who just got laid toni—" then, "wait, what's wrong?" just as the elevator door shuts in my face.

*Blyad'.*

DELICATE WRISTS I could easily hold in one hand. A tiny waist I could easily span with two. Long lovely legs wrapped around my ass while my hands were cupping hers. Her tongue moving in my mouth. Tasting her. Feeling how wet her pussy was under my fingers. Her hand on my cock. *Fuuuuck.*

Talia's body working with mine was a study in contrasts.

And it's the only thing I can think about as the lift takes me up three floors away from her. I wonder if she'll ever know just how badly I wanted to take her to bed and explore every inch of her finely made form. That kiss was just a taste. A small taste that only made me want to spend hours pleasuring her. More than I've ever wanted anyone before in my life.

What the fuck just happened?

Somehow—through a haze of frustration—I manage to stumble up to my apartment, stopping to bang my head against the door before unlocking it. I am an idiot. That was not good. I mean, it was good. Too good. But I did not handle it well. I should go back and explain myself. I wasn't trying to be a jerk. Far from it, in fact. I was trying to be respectful. I was trying not to take advantage of her.

I guess I shouldn't have announced I was going to kiss her. Bloody fucking hell. This is all my fault. I should go back and apologize. Get on my knees and beg her forgiveness. Or get on my knees and do something else to her instead...*because the scent of her is still on my fingers.*

No. I drew a line but crossed it. It's important I don't cross it again. I respect her too much and very much need her counsel. Somehow, I'll need to find a way to make this disaster up to her.

As soon as I get inside, I make a beeline for my shower. Priority number one is washing away all the grime I can feel on my skin right now. Maybe it can wash away the stupid thing I just did with Talia too. But that's totally wishful thinking because as soon as I step under the hot water filling my bathroom with steam, all I can see is Talia, twisting her hair around her finger as she read to me, her beautiful pink lips moving as she spoke. All I can feel is the softness of those lips pressed to mine as I nibbled on her bottom lip with my teeth, and how soft and wet her pussy was against my fingers underneath those smokin' hot leather pants.

My hand is on my cock before I can even stop myself. Jerking off in the shower is nothing new but doing it to thoughts of Talia is. I don't want to forget how she smelled and tasted and felt. Or the noises she made. Or the way she rubbed against me when I had her underneath me. Or how my cock felt in her tight grip. Talia is an intelligent woman, a successful woman. Her mind impresses me as much as anything else but tonight? I experienced another side of her: uncaged, wanton, and perfectly fucking gorgeous. I want more from her. Much, much more.

I come explosively, thinking only of her, gritting

my teeth and groaning loudly as the cum jets out the tip of my cock. I wish it was buried tight and deep inside her instead of being fisted in my hand. It's not enough, not by a million miles. But it has to be.

It has to be, because even if I wanted to go back for more, she'd never accept my lame excuse. Why I *had to pull away*. And she didn't deserve what I did; something that can't happen again. *Fuck.*

TYLER ELBOWS me in the ribs.

"I saw you leave, bro. Alone like some kind of celibate monk or whatever."

I grit my teeth and ignore him as I pull on my pads. He gets another jab in before I can get covered up. "Why are you so concerned about what I do or don't do in my private life?"

"I'm just sayin'" he rattles on, "that it's much nicer to get your threesome on with twins than to go home to your sad, empty apartment to whack off by yourself. You gotta live a little, buddy."

"You live your way, I'll live mine. I already told you casual is not my thing."

"Well, with a face like yours, it should be," he says with a shrug. "And I'm secure enough in my manhood to recognize when a dude is better lookin' than me. My bestie, Viktor? Not better looking than me. Evan K? Ehhh, yeah, maybe. You? Way outside of my sphere of hotness. It's a waste not to let such good looks work for you, man."

I can't help but laugh, even as I'm shaking my head. Tyler is ridiculous. And not far from the truth. I mean, I didn't technically go home alone, but I did whack off by myself. A hazard of getting too close to Talia Wentworth. Of course, Tyler doesn't need to know a single thing about her. No way do I want him even near her.

Dressed in my practice uniform I head out on the ice, my head still on the pretty girl with the glasses. I swear, she's been all I've been able to think about for the past two days. I really screwed things up with her and I still don't know what to do about it.

For two days, I've been messing up in practice because my head is not in the game like it should be. Coach has gotten on me for missing passes, letting myself get checked, and not hitting the goals I should be able to shoot with my eyes closed. And now, Evan is pulling me to the side.

"Dude, you want to tell me what's going on with you? You sick or something?"

"Something like that," I mutter, because I'm definitely not going to admit that my issues on the ice have to do with the fact that I kissed my investment advisor and liked it too much.

"Sit this drill out if you need to," he says.

I shake my head. "I'll get it together. Sorry."

Evan doesn't look convinced. He puts his gloved hand on my padded shoulder and says, "Take a break if you need it. Or we can talk after practice."

I give a nod and head off to grab water, banishing all thoughts of Talia for now. I do manage to get my head into the practice game as we scrimmage, my shots getting clearer. But I've got a pounding headache when I head back to the locker room afterwards.

Evan doesn't mess around and sends me straight to PT.

Pam has me face down on the table as she works at tense muscles in my shoulder and neck. "No wonder you've got a headache. There's a lot happening here."

"Yes, I have always carried tension there," I explain.

"We don't think this is concussion-related, do we?" she asks.

"No, it is not."

"Something going on that's stressing you out? Seems like the team is finally gelling pretty well."

My first inclination is to clam up. No one needs to know what a total *mudak* I was with Talia the other night. But it's really nagging at me, and maybe Pam would know how to help me make it right.

"The team is good." Groaning as she puts pressure on a particularly tight spot in my shoulder, I decide to share with her. "It's just that I think—ahh...I *know* I messed up...with a woman."

"Oh boy!" She becomes positively gleeful. "Well, lay it on me, pal. I'll tell you how deep you're in it and just what it'll take to dig yourself back out."

I let out a huff of breath through my nose. "Well, there is this woman. She is helping me to figure out my investments. Very smart. Very—"

"Beautiful?"

"Yes. Incredibly. But I can't cross the line with her. I really need her help with my money management situation, so I don't want to jeopardize our business relationship."

"But you did, I'd gather?"

"Yes. I saw her out at a club the other night. We danced and then I walked her home. It turns out we live in the same building, so we showed each other our apartments."

"That doesn't sound so bad," Pam says. "Turn over on your back for me."

I flip over and then continue with the story. I tell her about Talia spilling her tea on me. "She is always spilling things." I can't help chuckling. "So I had to take off my shirt, and then she read to me."

"She...read to you? Like, financial papers or something?"

"No, a fantasy novel." I can feel my face doing something between a grin and a wince. "It is a long story. But it...it was sexy. Her reading. And she looked so beautiful. Annnd...then I kissed her."

"And then she slapped your face and told you to go to hell?" Pam grins down at me.

"No, quite the opposite. She reciprocated. A lot."

"Okay, you were both into it. What's the problem?"

"She is my investment manager. I did not want to cross the professional line, but I did. So, I backed off, apologized, and left."

"Wait, so you kissed her, then rejected her?"

*And that's why you don't tell another woman about the idiot you were.* Because they tell it as it is. *Shameful.*

"I suppose it would appear so," I admit. "I just— the kissing was over the line in the first place. I didn't want to further complicate things between us. I thought I was doing the right thing by putting a halt on further intimacy."

"Hmmm."

Pam works at stretching my arms and shoulders while she thinks about what I've just told her. Finally, she tells me to sit up and asks how I'm feeling."

"Better. Thank you."

"You're welcome. So, I get where you're coming from. The team here has this crazy non-fraternization policy, which has been challenged in numerous ways over the past couple of years. Georg and I met before I started here, but things got more serious once I started working on staff and we really couldn't be together."

"But you are, so—"

"So, yeah. We let it happen, and sometimes in really not-smart ways, you know? We did bad things in this very room. Bad things that were captured on an audio recording." She lifts her eyebrows. "Not my proudest moment as a professional, being called in by my boss for screwing around with a player in my workspace."

"Ouch." I can't help wincing.

"I narrowly missed being fired. Georg got slapped

on the wrist. But, somehow, it all worked out and we're together and we still work here. The point is, I know a little bit about wanting what you're not supposed to have."

"Thank you for sharing that with me, Pam. Truly. But I still don't know what to do about Talia."

"Well, maybe this is oversimplifying, but what if you buy her some flowers and ask her on a proper date?"

"What about our professional relationship though?"

She shrugs. "I think it will all work itself out if it's meant to be. You like her, she likes you, there's got to be something worth exploring there. And if it doesn't work out, you're both adults and you can probably figure out how to continue to work together. I mean, shit, Georg and I only see our financial advisors a couple of times a year now. You'd barely have to see her if you really didn't want to."

"Thanks." I offer my knuckles for a fist bump. "For helping me."

"You're welcome." She bumps me back. "Keep me posted on how it goes with Talia."

I head out, Pam's advice swirling in my head. What if I did take her flowers and ask her on a proper date? I mean, Pam is right, I do like her. I know I'm very attracted to her, and she seemed attracted to me. Of course, it could have been the alcohol...

*Der'mo.* What if it was just the alcohol talking and now she very much regrets kissing me?

I need to think carefully about what to do next. Because I cannot fuck this up more than I already have with her.

# 20

# you should be his sex advisor, too

Talia

Ugh. I can't get my head into work stuff at all. My stomach is a flip-flopping disaster zone. My head hurts. My heart is racing. I'm not a panic attack kind of girl but this feels like one. Or maybe it's karma. Karma for getting all hot and bothered over yet another of my clients. What is wrong with me?

It's been three days since that hot mess with Boris, and I haven't heard a peep from him. I've been thinking about him, it, the situation. Ugh. Constantly. It just doesn't go away, the thinking or the wanting. And to add to my anxious misery, I'm still totally hot for the guy. Totally turned on and wanting nothing more than his big hard—

*Stop.*

Boris rejected me. He had a change of heart apparently and then totally bolted from my apartment.

But as he left, Parker came in and that's when I

completely lost my shit. Bawled like a teenage girl ditched on prom night. Seriously. Not just because he left. I think, probably, his leaving was the right thing to do. Still, it doesn't mean it felt good to watch him go, even though I know he was as turned on as I was. But when Parker came back in? I fell apart, collapsing into a weeping mess on the floor. I was literally sick for letting it go so far, for being such a sluttress. Because I was one. One-hundred-percent-out-of-control-sluttress-trying-to-bang-her-client. *How horrifyingly humiliating.*

He must think I'm so immature and unprofessional. I can't even brush it off like, "No big deal, we were drunk," because I wasn't drunk and he wasn't either. I was just my usual, awkward, idiot self, spilling tea on him. And then he was shirtless, and then he wanted me to read to him.

"Oh my God." I lean back in my chair and yell out loud into my empty office. "What an absolute fool I am!"

Boris was totally turned on by my reading. He looked like he literally wanted to devour me, like he might eat me alive. And, frankly, I wanted him to go there.

It's embarrassing that I let myself get so worked up, so out of control. And then he tells me he doesn't want to cross a professional line? *Already crossed it when you looked at me that way, buddy.* Crossed the fucking finish line when you kissed me.

It probably wasn't just professional courtesy that stopped him. I mean, he's an athlete. A gorgeous, chiseled work of art. He's famous and could probably have any woman he wanted. Why would he want some nerdy girl in thick glasses who can barely take a step without spilling something on herself or doing something weird?

I'm probably destined to be a spinster cat lady whose only hobby is reading long fantasy books—maybe knitting a throw blanket once in a while when I really want to spice things up a little. Note to self: Look into finding a "knitting cat lovers" group on Facebook to join.

At least there's my sweet little LuLu who loves me.

Of course, Parker had a totally different take on that night...

WHEN SHE WALKED IN, *I busted out in big, stupid tears of regret. I told her what happened, the whole weird scene, and then admitted how much I genuinely liked the guy.*

*"He's kind and sweet and quiet." I did my best to gulp back the tears but wasn't very successful. "He's not an arrogant prick like some of the sports stars we have to work with."*

*"Welp, I suggest you pull up your big girl panties, Talia my love, and go get him if you want him."*

*I hadn't wanted to admit how very much I wanted him, not even to Parker, my best friend in the whole world. But she knew, because she always knows.*

*"Look, I can see how hard you're fighting against this, and I get it," she said. "Believe me, I know what's*

*going on in that big brain of yours. You're thinking what a cluster your last client fraternization ended up being. But the fucker was married with children and just wanted a side piece. And you were young and inexperienced, and you thought it was something more."*

*"Not helping." I groaned and flopped back onto my chaise with great dramatic flair.*

*"Hear me out though. I'm just saying you got caught up in something he never meant to move forward. It happens to many a good human, but I need to remind you not everyone is a prick like that last guy."*

*"He has a name..." I started to say.*

*"No, he really doesn't," she replied, her lips doing the pursed, defiant thing they do when she's done taking someone's bullshit. "He doesn't get to have a name because he's a ghost. He's nobody to you anymore. And this guy? Boris? He's a real dude and he's obviously into you but too much of a gentleman to push it very far. But you know? Maybe it's meant to be?"*

*"He is a really good guy," I said, sniffling. "I looked him up. A lot."*

*I gave Parker a rueful, I-stalked-a-guy look and she laughed. "He's also totally single, right?" she asked.*

*"Totally. Not a one-night stand kind of guy, I've learned. Very honorable."*

*"And very hot," Parker said.*

*"That too," I replied.*

I THINK PARKER WAS RIGHT. Boris is a real man, and he's kind, and he pushes all my buttons.

And yes, he is my client, but maybe that doesn't matter so much...

"No, dumbass," I say to myself. "Of course it matters."

It won't be surprising to hear that I'm not very experienced with men. I dated a few guys in college, had sex maybe twice and frankly never figured out what the fuss was all about. And even with Cameron the sex was just okay. It didn't change my life or anything. I just enjoyed having someone who seemed to find me attractive. Lame. So very lame I know.

Now, as I try to get myself under some semblance of emotional control, I know that I just hadn't yet found someone who could make my motor hum, so to speak. And Boris got me from zero to sixty without doing much of anything at all. It was just a little taste, but now I want more. Now I want to experience what Parker has always gushed over. *Hot. Sensual. Fucking.* I want that, and I think Boris would have given it to me. *Shit. Shit. Shit.*

I stand up and shake my arms out, trying to will my body to calm down. I head into the tiny bathroom to wash my face, but just as I look up at myself in the mirror, I hear the little bell on my door jingle and the hairs on my arms stand straight up. I know it's him. I don't know how, but I just know it's Boris. My heart picks up its racing pace all over again.

What if he says *I* was the one who stepped over the line? I mean, I was practically humping his leg. Suddenly, I'm just really, really embarrassed, and I want nothing more than to jump into a very deep hole and starve rather than go out and face his consternation.

I take a quick, sharp breath and blow it back out, mentally preparing myself to get fired by Boris and, likely, by Harold once he finds out I've lost another important client because I can't control my hormones.

When I peek out, he's standing awkwardly in the middle of my office, looking gorgeous in a plain, gray T-shirt and jeans. His hands are shoved into his pockets, his strong shoulders hunched. I step out into view and his eyes go wide.

"I wasn't sure you were here, but the door was unlocked, so..."

My cheeks going hot, I take a deep breath in and hold it. I gesture to the chair and find my way to my own seat, legs wobbly as fuck. As soon as we both sit, I start talking. "I'm so ashamed of myself, Boris. You must be completely horrified by my behavior the other night. I just want to tell you—"

He puts up a hand and stops me. "No, Talia. It was me. I started it by kissing you. It is my fault. I am the one who is ashamed."

I bite my lip and look away. "Well, a few beers can make anyone look kissable, right?" I give a shrug and an awkward, nervous laugh.

"I don't know why you say such things. I don't drink often and certainly not to excess. I was sober. It was a choice, and I am sorry I crossed the line with you."

"Wait, you're sorry?" I'm dumbfounded. "Why

would *you* be sorry? You weren't the one acting like an animal in heat."

I can see Boris's lips quirk. He puts his hand to his mouth and fakes a cough to keep from laughing. "I think there is more to talk about when it comes to this thing between us, but I want to start by telling you I called my financial advisors in Russia and they should be transferring all of the information about my accounts to you by end of week."

"You still want to have me manage your investments?" I'm sure the shock is written all over my face. "I thought you were here to fire me."

This time it's Boris who looks shocked, his strong brows shooting up into his hairline. "Why would you think that? I need you."

"You need me?"

"I need your help. I trust you. I very much want to continue working with you."

"Oh." I don't really know how to feel right now but I force myself into a more professional posture, back straight, legs crossed, as I look at my computer just to avoid meeting his gaze. I don't want him to see that I'm at war. Yes, I want his business, but I also want him. And hearing him say he needs me...I should be happy, but the disappointment is there, because it's my financial mind he needs, and nothing more. *But, of course, Talia. He said lovely words about me being beautiful, but they weren't really true.* He wants my brain. Nothing surprising there. "I shouldn't have stepped over the line. I apologize. But yes, of course, I'd love to continue to work for you."

Boris opens his mouth and then closes it again. His mouth is a razor, set tight. It takes him a minute to figure out what to say.

"Talia, I truly blame myself for this. I am so sorry that I made you feel I would not want to continue our professional relationship."

"No, it's—I'm just—it's me. I was the crazy one. I don't want you to feel badly at all."

"I do, though. I actually came here with a secondary motive to ask you on a proper date, but I suppose, considering how this conversation is going, maybe I should not?"

This time, my mouth drops open. "What? You want to go on a date...with me?"

"I thought perhaps—"

"Wait. *You* cut things off the other night. *You* walked away. Now you want to ask me out? Isn't that running a little hot and cold, Boris?"

He sits back in his seat. "I'm sorry. I did not mean to offend you."

I put a hand up. "No. I'm not offended, but I am confused. You bolted like you were the one offended the other night and now—"

Boris stands quickly, nearly knocking over the chair. "Never mind. Let's just keep it professional, then."

I grit my teeth. "Okay, whatever," I manage to say. "That's fine. But sit back down. We have business to finish up."

Angry and hurt, I walk Boris through everything I need from his Russian investment managers and talk him through everything we need to do on this end to ensure a smooth transition. We already have accounts set up with his current wages, so I just need a small amount of paperwork to prepare for the transfer of overseas accounts. I read everything to him and make sure he understands before having him sign. Even though this thing between us is a total cluster—as Parker noted—I still want to ensure he doesn't get *or feel* screwed again. He doesn't deserve it.

Once we're done, he stands and reaches out a hand for me to shake. It feels forced and formal and I hate it. But I take his offer reluctantly, and probably wearing an expression akin to what one might wear when he or she has smelled a dead fish. Still, when we touch, there's a zing of energy that goes right to my core. It's that easy and I know he feels it, too, because his eyes go wide and he pulls away quickly, clearing his throat and saying goodbye before making a hasty retreat.

In the end I decide not to dwell on it. Well, I dwell on it a little, kicking myself for not being nicer when he said he wanted to ask me on a date. He caught me off guard and I'm not proud of the way I responded. Well crap.

Still, I have work to do. A career to maintain. And I can at least report that I have not lost Boris's business when I call Harold later.

"Hey, Talia, he says. "How's Sin City this week?"

"Sinful," I say.

"Good to hear," he says. "More sin means more money will need investing."

"True. I do have good news on that front."

"The sinning or the investing?"

"The investing, duh," I say. "The Ice Dragon is moving all of his Russian puck money to us, to add in with the new accounts we set up for his Crush contract."

"Puck money." He chuckles. "Cute. I love it, and really good news, T. The whole shebang, huh?"

"Yep. We'll see how it all shakes out. These guys were screwing him royally. I can get it under control, but I need to see what they send to me first. I'm sure they'll try to fuck him over one more time before losing his business."

"Well, let me know if we need to call in the lawyers."

"Will do, chief."

"Congrats. He's a big name to land. You're killin' it out there. Glad I sent you."

"It was a good move for both of us," I answer. "Hey, what do you know about Boris?"

"Why? He creeping you out?"

"No, not at all. He seems really decent, but I know sometimes we can't judge by the wrapper."

"Scott tells me he's a good dude," Harold says. "Quiet. Not a big partier. Not a womanizer. Kind of boring by pro athlete standards. His words."

"And as a player? He worth the hype?"

"Haven't you watched his highlights?"

"Some," I say, not wanting to admit that it's the still photos of him shirtless that seem to garner my attention lately. And my skin burns just thinking how hot and strong and yes, sexy, touching him had been.

"He's courteous, a good sportsman. Strong player, super consistent. He scores like crazy. With Evan on the wing...damn. The Crush is definitely favored to take the Cup this season."

"And the Russian connection?"

"Some shady ties, but that's kind of par for the course, to mix my sports metaphors. All those guys who played Russian puck are tied to some dark characters, either directly or indirectly. It's Russia, you know? Boris somewhat less than most, though."

"Okay," I say. "Thanks. He seems great. Just wanted to confirm. I'll let you know when the transfers are all in place."

We hang up and I put my head down and force myself to get some work done. Still, I find myself edgy and cranky by five, so I knock off earlier than usual with plans to get a giant, messy sandwich made of all the meats and then take it home so I can feed my feelings in private.

I wander down the street to a little deli that has fast become one of my favorites, heading straight to the counter to order a Rueben with extra meat. I pay and stand to the side, waiting for my food, as a familiar-looking guy wanders in, sunglasses on even though he's inside.

He stares at the board for a long time before placing his order. When he steps near me, he lifts his sunglasses and stares at me with piercing blue eyes, lots of tats peeking out of his collar and shirt sleeves.

He looks young. Blond and fit, and it occurs to me that I've seen this guy at the arena.

"Do I know you?" he asks.

"No, but you play for the Crush, right?"

He nods and extends a hand. "Tyler."

"Talia." I shake his hand.

He considers me for a second then it dawns on him. He laughs softly. "I know those glasses. You're the hot librarian who was looking for Boring Boris that one day. And the one he was drooling over at the club the other night."

"He wasn't drooling. Come on."

He shrugs and makes a face that says otherwise. "He was being a class-B creeper, looking at you from afar for the longest time. Took no interest in any of the many tasty treats I tried to feed him through the night."

"That sounds sexist." I can't help cringing.

"It sounds like a compliment, lady. He was all about you and only you, even though I know he didn't leave with you. Poor sap-bastard probably fell asleep with his cock in his hand and a sexy nerd on his mind."

I've been around a lot of crude men, men who think they can say and do whatever they want. This guy ranks up there, though I suppose he thinks he's just being funny. And I'm not very good at hiding my true feelings.

"Well, that's not exactly true," I say. "He did walk me home. We live in the same building. But I'm his financial advisor. Nothing more."

"Well, I know the guy only had eyes for you. He absolutely made it clear he wasn't into one-night stands, no matter how hard I tried to find him a hookup. He's a terrible wingman. You should be his sex advisor, too. He needs a good doink or his game's gonna suffer. Just sayin'."

My sandwich comes up, and I'm almost feel too queasy from my conversation with Tyler to take it, but the bag is already greasy, just the way I like it. No man comes between me and my meat sandwiches. I grab it and bolt, getting a distracted goodbye as Tyler's phone rings.

I walk home, thinking about what Tyler said. Boris only had eyes for me? All night? And he's definitely, totally not into one-night stands? I guess I probably knew that about him. He's very upstanding that way. Maybe he pushed me away because he thought it wouldn't be meaningful if we took it too far that night? Maybe he wanted more than just a hot, quick screw? Maybe his awkwardness today was because he genuinely wanted to take me on a date, to get to know me before we...

I blow a frustrated breath out as I reach my building. I'm such an idiot. I clearly have no business trying to be with anyone, because I cannot read social cues. This has always been my problem. I'm not fixated on my looks or on whether or not someone finds me pretty or whatever. I'm smart and I am who I am. I can't change it. But I do think I miss signs sometimes. Once, Cameron told me I was beautiful after a meeting, and I thought it was a broad compliment because I'd just told him his investments did well for the quarter. It was much later he finally came right out and said, "I'm hitting on you, are you not getting it?"

I was not getting it. And now I wish I'd never gotten it. But whatever. Water under the bridge and all that. But Boris? Boris isn't water under the bridge. Not for me. I need to fix this with him. He's worth it to at least try.

I think about all the crude things Tyler said and I'm still shaking my head as I step off the elevator on my floor, ready for my pajamas, and my cat, and a book, and this greasy sandwich that's going to taste so amazing...*Oh my God. Fuck.*

But none of those things happen because my door is open a quarter of an inch. I push it open tentatively, finding the inside completely ransacked. My many books are strewn all over the floor, askew in ways that make my little bibliophile's heart hurt. My kitchen drawers have been emptied. My chaise is flipped upside down.

My heart is beating so hard in my chest. All I can do is stare at the mess. "Who would do this? Who in the hell would do this?" I sob. And then, "Where's LuLu?"

# 21
# ice dragon is not yours

Boris

T'm sitting on my couch watching baseball highlights on ESPN when there's a loud, frantic banging on my door. I get up and head to the door, swinging it open to find a teary, hyperventilating Talia there. She's got her work bag on her shoulder and a greasy sandwich bag in one hand.

"Talia, what—"

"My apartment's been ransacked. Everything is everywhere." Her words are a steady, breathless stream. "I'm afraid to go in by myself and I didn't see LuLu and—"

Her chin shakes as her face screws into a mixture of fear and anger and worry. I reach out and pull her into a hug as she sobs into my shirt. When she pulls away, I hold her face in my hands. "Let's go down and check it out together."

I grab my keys and throw on some flip-flops, following her out into the hallway.

A few minutes later, we're peering into the mess of

her apartment. Books and papers are strewn all over. Everything that was sweet with Talia the other night has been upended and destroyed. What the hell?

"LuLu?" she says, her voice cracking. "LuLu? Baby kitty?"

When the cat doesn't appear, Talia sinks to the floor, breaking into sobs. I do the best thing I can think of, starting to pick up books, placing them back on the shelves. I know she's probably got a system but for now, I think it's just important to get things cleaned up and feeling more normal. Talia just cries silently from her place by the door—that is, until a small meow sounds from the rear of the apartment. Talia jumps up, scrambling toward the sound. A moment later, I can hear her telling the cat how worried she was.

Talia returns to the main room, a fluffy white cat in her arms. She meets my gaze and I see the relief in her eyes. "I can deal with losing stuff, you know? But LuLu?" She doesn't finish the thought. Her eyes brim with tears again and I stand helplessly, not sure how to respond. I've never had a pet. I don't know what it's like to have something that means so much to me. To be so worried about another person or an animal's safety.

"The two of you are perfect together," I say quietly.

"We are indeed." Talia rubs noses with LuLu and gives a relieved sigh.

After snuggling her cat for a few minutes, Talia takes a deep breath, squares her shoulders, and heads to the door, shutting it and rolling up the sleeves of her blouse. She starts working in the kitchen while I continue to replace books on the shelves. We work in silence for a very long time; the cat sniffing around and rubbing against my legs every so often. I get the books shelved and then move to flip the chaise upright. When I do, a piece of paper flutters to the floor.

On it are those magazine cut-out letters like serial killers make. I look at it quizzically, the differently shaped and colored letters really messing with my dyslexic brain. Whatever it is, it can't be good. Talia looks over, sees my face, and then makes her way to my side, grabbing the piece of paper from my hands.

"Do not accept the transfer. Ice Dragon is not yours to manage. Your only warning," she reads. Her eyes flit up to mine and her hands start to shake.

"Ice Dragon," I repeat. "This has to do with me?"

"I'd wager the guys who've been ripping you off all these years don't like the idea of losing their cash cow."

"But why would they threaten you? I am the one who came to you. I made this choice to move my money."

"But I'm the one who stands to gain from this, while they lose. Plus, I'm a woman and they think I'll be scared and back down."

"*Ublyudok!*" I swear in Russian. Then, "Sorry."

Talia gives me a look that is both questioning and amused. "I assume that's a swear word you're apologizing for?"

"It was, sorry."

"Well, there's no reason to be. This situation is more than worth a few swears."

"I'm also sorry this happened because of me, Talia. I had no idea."

"I get that." She clears her throat nervously.

I bite the inside of my lip. "This makes no sense. It's business. Why would they make any kind of threats?"

"Really?" she asks. "Boris, I told you they've been ripping you off. Funneling money away from your accounts for years to the tune of maybe millions of dollars. They had a sweet gig going until I came along and figured them out."

"But you did not tell them you knew what they were doing?"

She shrugs. "I may have mentioned my concerns to Vlad. I can't remember."

My shoulders droop and I rub my forehead, where a headache is blooming again. "This is not good, Talia. What should we do?"

"Call the police?" she asks.

I look around. "Should we have cleaned up?"

"Probably not. Crime scene one-oh-one, right?"

I push my lips to one side. "Oops."

The police arrive quickly. The first thing Talia does is apologize for cleaning up the mess. They give her a lecture about it, and she snaps, her patience clearly at an end. "Yeah, I know, we realized we should have called you all first and left things alone."

After telling her story, the police ask me about my role in the situation. I explain what I saw, and what I think is going on. We hand over the note and the police dust a few surfaces for fingerprints before leaving us alone again, telling Talia they'll follow up with her soon.

"Did you want to eat your sandwich?" I ask, pointing to the greasy bag that's still where she left it on the floor by the door.

She laughs. It's a hysterical, short sound that makes my chest feel funny. I rub the spot absently with my fingertips as she walks over to pick up the bag. Holding it up between two fingertips, she looks absolutely drained. "All I wanted was to curl up with this big, meaty sandwich and a book." She pouts.

"Plans thwarted."

"Fucking annoying."

I don't bother hiding the smirk at her potty mouth. "Well, I have not eaten yet, either. Why don't we go back to my apartment and order some sandwiches for delivery?"

"Okay," she says. I can see there's something else on her mind.

"What?"

"I just...I feel really nervous sleeping here alone tonight. They got into my house, Boris. They could have hurt LuLu. Hurt me." I can see her lip wobbling.

"Bring some things with you then and you can stay with me. I'll sleep on the couch."

"Are you sure?"

"Of course. I mean, I get it. I wouldn't feel safe here now either. Tomorrow we can get a security system installed."

"And LuLu? Can she come? I can bring her litter box to your place. She's a good girl and will use it, promise—"

I hold a hand up. "Of course, Talia. I would love to have both of you ladies as my guests for as long as you need."

She mouths "thank you" and seems to breathe a sigh of relief before grabbing a few things from her closet and bathroom. She shoves her stuff into tote bag along with her laptop and then gathers up LuLu's supplies in another big bag. I carry the bags as she scoops up LuLu into her arms and we head out. I follow behind her, making sure to shut and lock the door with the keys she left hanging in the lock from when she first came home.

"I **NEED** every paper you have relating to your investments." LuLu takes off as soon as she's set down, eager to sniff her way around a new space, as Talia pulls her long blonde hair into a ponytail with a stretchy band from her wrist.

The minute we are all inside my apartment, Talia transforms into a coiled spring of energy. I knew she was smart but this small act—pulling back her hair and jumping into action—shows me she's tough, too. Not about to let this situation make her feel intimidated, I nod and head to the bedroom, pulling a box of investment paperwork from the top shelf of my closet. She folds herself onto my living room floor and opens it up, pulling out papers, scanning, organizing. She takes notes and jots numbers on a scrap piece of paper.

Not sure what I can do to help her, I call to replace the deli sandwich she was so looking forward to, heading out to pick it up, only to return fifteen minutes later to find her in the same position, the same look of determination on her pretty face.

I hand her the sandwich to which she says, "Thanks," barely looking up from her work. When she pulls out the sandwich, loaded with double meat as per the shop owner's recommendation when I mentioned who I was ordering for, she inhales deeply, sighs happily, and then takes a huge, sloppy bite that ends up dripping onto her lap.

"Well, shit," Talia says, looking down at the glob of dressing and meat and sauerkraut that now rests on her thigh. She's nothing like the skinny puck bunnies who not only would never eat like that in front of a guy but would probably scream bloody murder if a big glob of greasy food fell in their lap. But when Talia does it? Adorable. I'm shaking my head when I grab a bunch of paper towels and hand them to her, unable to suppress my laughter. She says, "Shut it, Ice Dragon," but then she laughs, too.

I pace for a while, before she tells me to go get her some Ben & Jerry's. Tells me, not asks me. And I'm happy to follow orders because it gives me something to do besides fret. And I don't really even know what I'm fretting about, other than the fact that Talia's apartment was ransacked because of me.

Honestly, I feel powerless and it's a shitty feeling to have. So I head out to get the ice cream she ordered, some fudgy kind with pretzels in it. I have to go to three stores before I find it and I'm gone for an hour. But when I return, she looks up at me, eagle-eyed and serious, and says, "I don't have a final number but from what I can tell, these guys siphoned about three million dollars, possibly more from you since you were eighteen years old."

You could probably push me over with a feather. "Siphoned? You mean fees?"

Talia levels me with a *No, dummy* kind of look and says, "No, the fees are exorbitant on their own. That's another million, probably, but they also sent money to offshore accounts that are not in your name. They're not tax shelters but they're made to look like they are. They were stealing from you, because they knew you wouldn't delve into the details."

I feel totally and completely shell-shocked as I go over to my couch and flop down, my legs suddenly feeling weak. No wonder my finances are never as good as they should be. No wonder I feel like I'm not getting anywhere. I'm not.

"I feel so stupid right now," I say, more to myself than to Talia.

"The ultra-risky investments were a smokescreen, Boris," she answers. "They were meant to make it look like the losses were part of the risk. Only someone really poring over this stuff would find it. I saw it right away but if you didn't have anyone advocating for you, how would you know?"

"They approached me when I was young, just starting to make money." My voice sounds distant to my own ears. "They treated me like I was a special customer. I felt like I was hot stuff back then, you know? I trusted them."

"You shouldn't beat yourself up about it, though. You were just a boy, and no one was there to help you read the fine print or think over the plan. Anyone could have fallen into this trap. Anyone probably did. You can't be the only player these guys stole from. There are certainly more guys just like you being ripped off right now by people just like them. Corrupt financial management is very common in professional sports where clients are kept in the dark about their money and taken advantage of."

"I really am not sure what to do about this," I admit.

"It's out of our league, for sure," Talia answers, standing and stretching, her limbs unfurling like a cat. She steps toward me and plucks the pint of ice cream and plastic spoon from my hands. "I'm going to go take a bath, eat my feelings, and think of a plan though."

I stand helplessly as she wanders off to make herself comfortable. It's not until I hear the bath running that I finally sink into the nearest chair, weary and worried.

# 22
# why do you do that?

Talia

Look at me, acting like I own the place. I found some minty-smelling body wash that made for a good makeshift bubble bath. As I soak, I'm shoving Ben & Jerry's into my face like there's not going to be a tomorrow. The eating is the only thing keeping me from throwing up with worry and anxiety. I know that sounds weird, but whatever, it works.

But this investment situation is not good. Not good at all. These guys are criminals, thieves, threatening possible violence, and just plain taking advantage because nobody has ever stepped in to prevent them.

Poor Boris. He's lost millions to them. He's worked hard to build his career and he trusted these people. Hell, I think he trusts everyone and anyone, if I'm being honest. He's so good, and he does not deserve this. I have to help him make this right. At the very least, I can protect his future earnings. That's something. But still, we can't just let these guys intimidate and bully us. We can't just let them get away with it.

I'll call Harold in the morning. I'll tell him what happened and ask him to help me figure out what to do, who to call. There has be police or other authorities who can help in this kind of situation with a foreign government, right?

When I finish thinking and soaking and overindulging, I let out the water and slip out of the tub, wrapping a giant, soft towel around me. It smells like Boris. Masculine and woodsy and yum. It takes me straight back to that night at my apartment. The kissing and the touching we did.

Oh boy. I don't need to go there. I don't need to be thinking about the feel of his lips, or his hard body. Nope. Especially when I'm going to be sleeping in his apartment.

I peek my head out the door and, seeing no sign of him, I run across the hall into Boris's room, quickly pulling a T-shirt and pajama bottoms from my hastily packed bag. I use my finger to brush through my wet hair, then pull the Iain Cooper book from my bag, ready to forget break-ins and Russian investors, and all that stolen puck money for a moment. I just want to recede into a fantasy world for a while.

I walk back out to the living room with the book, thinking maybe Boris will want me to read to him again, or maybe he will want the mental break, too. I don't expect to find him lying on the couch with LuLu spread out on his chest. I sit at his feet and reach out, petting my cat, who totally ignores me. I can't lie—my heart melts a little. LuLu does not just automatically like people, but she's trusted Boris from day one.

"Traitor," I say.

Boris grins. "I think she likes me."

"I can see that."

"How was your bath?" Boris asks as he strokes his big hand down LuLu's back and then her tail in a long sweep.

"Not as relaxing as I'd hoped," I answer. "But I brought that book from last time, *Leaving Area 51*? Want me to read from it again?"

Boris nods, so I start reading from where I left off before, on the night we kissed. I read probably three chapters before I look up, and Boris is again looking at me in the most intimate way. His eyes are dark, his expression one of hunger. I meet his gaze, biting my bottom lip, not sure what to do or say.

"Should I keep reading?" There's a hitch in my throat so it comes out like a husky whisper. Boris keeps staring and it makes me tingly all over. My abdomen is suddenly flooded with heavy want. My nipples are tight buds beneath my thin T-shirt. It makes me feel so awkward. So what do I do? I blurt out, "What are you staring at?"

"You," he says, his voice low and thick. "You're the most beautiful woman I've ever seen, Talia."

I scoff, looking back down at my book as I feel my cheeks flush with heat. "That is not true."

"I don't know what you see in the mirror, but I see hair that looks like it was made of rare metal. And skin like cream. Perfect bow-shaped lips. And you're so smart. Way too smart for me, probably."

My breath is caught in my chest at the kind things he's saying, but it's that last statement that breaks my heart. "You're not dumb, Boris. You have dyslexia and we can get someone to help you with it. But you're not dumb. You're kind. A gentleman. And pretty gorgeous AF, too."

Boris sits up and LuLu lets out a noise of protest before hopping down to the floor. But Boris barely notices my cat, because his eyes are on my lips. On the hard pearls standing out against the fabric of my shirt. There is so much longing in his gaze that I nearly combust. No one has ever looked at me this way. Ever. I get it. I see it. This connection between us is real. It's a fast-moving train and there is nothing we can do to stop it.

Despite that, I need to get something off my chest. It's probably not the right time but I feel compelled. I need him to know the truth.

"I slept with a client once. We had an affair for weeks. And then I found out he was married with kids. Like, happily married. And I was so devastated. Felt so stupid. I was dreadfully embarrassed, and Harold sent me here so that I wouldn't be in the office, seeing Cameron all the time and making shit even more awkward for everyone."

"You did not know he was married before you started the affair?" Boris asks.

"No. He never wore a ring. And I was so inexperienced...dazzled by him. By the fact that someone like him would even find me remotely attractive."

"Why do you do that?"

"Do what?"

"Diminish yourself."

The weight of his words makes me blush even deeper. "I guess... I mean, I've always been smart, you know? Intimidatingly so for some, probably. And a bit of an ugly duckling. I just—"

"Wow."

"Wow, what?"

"Well, you've impressed me so much, Talia. Since I met you, you were so assured of your skills, your capacity to think through complex financial and investment details. The way you showed your resolve in the face of intimidation earlier tonight. To call yourself an ugly duckling...it is not at all in line with the way I view you."

"Thank you," is all I can think to say.

"I see why you are so worried about what this is between us," Boris answers. "And there is something. I'm not imagining it, right?"

"You're not," I say. "But—"

"But you can't do it again?"

"I'm sorry. I want you. I won't lie to you, Boris. But I also can't go through that again. You're a client and I'm committed to that. And if we took it somewhere, I feel it would just make things icky and complicated, especially when it doesn't work out. I can't take that humiliation again. Not when it comes to the job I love."

Boris looks like he wants to disagree, and part of me wants him to. Part of me wants him to say it will work out, that this is real, that it won't affect my job. Part of me—a big part—wants him to take me and kiss me and tell me not to worry about those things. That this is different. I know he's not Cameron. I feel so much more with Boris. The want is deeper. The desire is stronger. I feel the pull and I know he does too. And I know I'm pushing him away, but I want him to pull me back.

He doesn't, though. He just nods and says, "I understand, Talia. I want you to be happy." And then he lies down, turns to his side, and closes his eyes.

"Goodnight," I say quietly, feeling short of breath and damn near ready to cry. I stand and tiptoe into his bedroom, crawling into his bed that surrounds me in his delicious scent.

A scent that keeps me awake and longing for most of the night.

# 23
# taking care of business

Boris

"Hello, Ally, it is Boris." I have finally broken down and called Ally to get her started on my "life management," as Talia has described it.

"Oh, hi," she says. "I thought maybe you had changed your mind about hiring me."

"That fact that I have not called you sooner is just proof how badly I need the assistance. We will start to travel soon, and I really need you to help me get organized. Could we meet for coffee?"

When we do meet up at the coffee shop the next morning, I don't show up empty-handed. I've brought a substantial pile of bills and papers in a large file box. When I sit it in front of her, she raises her eyebrows. "What's this?"

"This is a box of bills and contracts and other miscellaneous life papers."

"And you want me to organize it?"

"Organize it. Help me set up recurring online payments. Read through and tell me anything that needs attention or discussion. I'm going to give you the key to my mailbox and I want you to manage it all."

"Okay, I can do that. Why the sudden focus on this?"

"I am trying to move all of my financial investments to Talia's firm as you know. Her apartment was ransacked after my current investment managers in Russia got word that I would be transferring my funds."

"Oh my God, no. Is she okay?"

"Yes, thankfully she wasn't hurt. But she was spooked. Apparently, they did not want to lose me as a customer."

"That's quite an excessive reaction."

"And they were taking a very large cut for a very long time. Unauthorized cuts."

"Ahh…that's not good."

"I have been too trusting for too long. The dyslexia makes it harder for me, of course, and so I need people who can watch my back. Talia is doing that for my financial investments. Can you do this for my daily life?"

"Yes, I can."

"Good. Can you work with Talia to see how we can best manage getting you paid, and how she recommends managing bill payments and such?"

"I can but, Boris?"

"Yes?"

"I don't mean to overstep, but..."

"Just ask me whatever you were going to say."

"There are resources out there that could help you with your dyslexia. Would you like me to research some things for you?"

I sit back in my chair and run my hands through my hair. "I have managed for a very long time."

"And, per your own acknowledgment, you have been ripped off for a long time too. I really don't want to make you uncomfortable. It's just that it seems like you might feel more...in control if you could manage it. A bit."

I think for a moment, then agree to let her do some research. Ally takes my box of papers and my mailbox key and heads off, with a promise to check in tomorrow.

PRACTICE IS BRUTAL, made up of two solid hours of drill work. We're not far out from our first preseason games and we're running like a machine. I feel much better about the way we play together in practice—I just hope it translates when the pressure is on in a regular game.

We head from the ice to the gym for strength and conditioning. I put in an hour on the treadmill, followed by a one-hour CrossFit-designed circuit. I'm literally dripping with sweat when I realize I have a PT appointment with Pam. A quick shower first is a must. Pam will thank me for not coming to her stinking of sweat.

She has me working on some range of motion for my shoulder when she casually slips in a question about how things went with Talia.

"No go," I say. "We both sort of stepped back and realized we should keep our relationship professional. There are a lot of things going on and it seemed like dating would be a definite complication."

"But do you like each other?"

"Yes, I like her very much."

"Then the 'keep it professional' excuse is baloney," she says, making little quote marks with her fingers in the air.

"How is it baloney?"

"Look, I work here, and Georg works here. Scarlett works here and Viktor works here. Evan's wife, Holly, used to work here doing Scarlett's job before she had her second kid. We all make it work, even though there can be professional crossover. She's your investment agent and you trust her with your wealth. Why wouldn't you trust that she can be an adult about trying a relationship?"

"I do trust her. Look, she told me she once had an affair with a married client. She did not know he was married at the time, but she was very hurt by the experience. She moved here to avoid being embarrassed by it and to start over. She does not want to make the same mistake twice."

"Are you married?"

"What? No."

"Then what's the problem? It's not the same thing."

"I already told you she doesn't want to cross lines between her business and personal life. She is building her career here and she doesn't want to have a reputation."

"Did she say that? She doesn't want to have a reputation?" Pam's arms are folded beneath her breasts and she wears a look that makes me think she's calling bullshit.

"No, she did not say those exact words. She said she doesn't want to be humiliated again, and that she couldn't take the risk of things being 'icky and complicated,' I say, making the little finger quotes like Pam did a minute ago.

"Okay." She motions for me to lie down and starts the massage portion of the session. "So, I get she's gun-shy and I get that you want to respect her wishes, but I also *know* when you find someone good, you should hold on tight to that person. I think you two can work it out, I really do, Boris."

I don't say anything in response. In fact, I am quiet for the remainder of the therapy session.

But I hope against hope Pam is right, because I want more with Talia. Now, whenever Pam compares the relationships I've seen my friends in, all I can see is Talia. Her wacky sense of humor, her bravery against adversity, her honesty even when it's hard, and her heart. Fuck, her heart. I want that in my life... daily. And I can see it, but how do I get it?

"VLAD," I say through the phone. "It's Boris."

"The Ice Dragon!" he yells. "How good to hear from you."

"My new investment manager's house got broken into. A note was left, warning her not to take my accounts." Vlad better be the good guy in this, as I've trusted him for years, too. Perhaps, time will tell, but I refuse to sound weak to him about this. About Talia.

Vlad is quiet for a moment. His jovial tone has disappeared completely when he finally responds. "They are feeling protective of the relationship they have built with you."

"Relationship?" I laugh. "It is not much of a relationship when they have been stealing money from me all these years."

"Now, Boris, those are serious allegations, friend."

"I am not your friend, and it is a fact. They have stolen millions from me over the years. However, I need you to do something for me that only you are qualified to do. Call your fixers on the ground in Las Vegas, or whatever you have to do to make it happen. I want those *ublyudki* to stay the hell away from Natalia Wentworth. If they want to come at me, fine, but she is just doing what I have asked her to do. I want you to figure out what these guys need to back away and move *my* money without problems."

"These things are complicated," Vlad says cryptically, "but I'll see what I can do. I'll contact

Heisenberg and fill him in on the situation. He is in Vegas and coordinates jobs for me from time to time.

"Thank you."

I hang up with him on my way to knock on Talia's apartment door.

She opens, dressed in a T-shirt and shorts that make her legs look very long. I have to force myself to stop staring and admiring which is no easy feat.

"Hey," she says. "Come on in."

"Did the security system come?" I ask, looking around. Her apartment is back to normal, everything in its place, or at least in whatever place Talia wants it to be in. She's slept at my apartment the last two nights, waiting until I could get here and install the security system she ordered.

In answer to my question, she points to a box by the door." That's probably it."

I open the box, pulling out the components for the do-it-yourself system, along with the instructions. I stare at the words as they jump all over the page, then turn to find Talia staring at me with a frown on her face.

"Let me read the directions?"

I nod and hand over the paper. She reads the instructions step by step as I complete the tasks, and in just over an hour, we have the whole system installed and working.

"Wow, they say it is a simple install and it really is," I comment.

"Hopefully it works like they say it will," she

answers. "Thanks for your help. I bet you'll be happy to have your bed back tonight."

"It was no bother," I tell her with a shrug. And it wasn't. Having her in my house, even LuLu, provided something I hadn't realized I'd been missing. Conversation. *Company.* "The main box has a camera and works with the Wi-Fi to call for help if someone forces entry. There are sensors on the windows, and there's a panic button in the bathroom. That should do it."

"Yep. I guess that should do it."

An awkward silence stretches between us. I don't know what's going on in Talia's mind, but my mind is thinking about how much I loved having her in my space. How I wish I could have shared my bed with her.

She clears her throat and says, "I got Ally's paperwork figured out and her payments set up. I agree with what I think was your concern and wouldn't give her access to bank account information, even to set up payments. I'd like to suggest that maybe you two sit down together where you log-in and then she can add the auto bill payments, or she can lead you through it? That way she doesn't see any of your passcodes, you know? It's not that I don't trust her, but in light of what we're dealing with, I just feel like it's better to be safe than sorry."

I nod. I don't know Ally well, but I sense that she's trustworthy. Still, Talia is right. I've been burned out of millions of dollars, so I can't be too careful right now.

She sees my hesitation and says, "We'll figure out a way to make it all work."

I sense she's talking about more than finances, but I don't have a response for her, so I just say, "Ally seems eager to get started, and with all that's happened, I feel like it's important to get organized as soon as possible. Thank you for suggesting the help. You were right, I do need it."

She shrugs. "I hope we picked the right person. When I spoke to her the other day, it felt like maybe she was taking too much ownership too quickly. I sense she's developed a little crush on you."

I let out a noise of disbelief. "Come on."

"No, I can hear it in her voice when she talks about you."

"Talia, she has been nothing but professional with me so far. And you're the one who wanted me to hire her. I was just trying to make you happy."

"That's dumb."

"Why is it dumb?" I cross my arms across my chest, annoyed by her suggestion.

"Why would you hire a person, pay money to a person, just to make your financial advisor happy?"

"Because my financial advisor is someone I trust. Because I take her suggestions seriously and appreciate all she's doing to help me. If she thinks hiring someone to help organize my life will help my financial well-being in the future, then that is what I'll do."

Talia's mouth quirks a little at my answer. "Well, your financial advisor only wants what's best for you."

Her tone is flirty and sexy, and I don't think she even realizes it. I have to will my cock not to respond. She has no idea—no fucking idea—how much I want her.

"And your client only wants to make you happy. And for you to be safe," I answer, trying to keep it light when I'm really fighting to stay under control. I can hear it in my own voice, the darkness, the want. I clear my throat, but I can't look away. "I'll fire her if you want me to."

"No," she says quickly. "No, you should keep her if you want her."

"I don't *want* her, Talia. I mean, I think she can help me with organization but the only person I really *want* is you."

Talia's chest moves like she's fighting to keep her breath even. I can see her nipples are hard, pressing against her T-shirt. I have to suppress the groan that nearly escapes when she licks her lips again. Christ.

"Well"—she takes a slow step toward me—"I want to thank you again for your help these last few days. I'd never have gotten through this without you."

A wave of relief rolls over me, glad our conversation has turned away from this tension, or whatever the fuck this is right now. "You wouldn't be in this mess if not for me. I owe it to you."

"You don't owe me anything," she says softly, her eyes boring into me as she takes another step closer.

"I do, Talia. I owe you a lot. Especially an apology—"

And then her lips are on mine, shutting me up in the best way possible. A hard, punishing kiss spilling over with heat and passion, maybe even some anger, and tasting of mint and chocolate.

My reaction is to take her cheeks in my hands and kiss her right back. Wild and desperate, a tangle of tongues and scrapes of teeth. There's nothing soft or gentle about it. But it's hot.

Insanely hot. Having Talia against me...to feel and touch and kiss.

### Talia

I TOOK a chance and just went for it. I kissed Boris.

He doesn't seem to mind even though he does growl a little when I tug our lips apart. "I've wanted to do that for a long time," I say, looking up at him.

"I've wanted to do a lot of things for a long time," he answers, his hands traveling from the cheeks of my face to the cheeks of my ass. *Umm, yeah.* Domineering Boris is super hot. He pulls me hard against him like he can't get me close enough. "You sleep in my bed and all I want is to join you there," he rasps on a hot breath.

"I would have let you," I tell him as he goes back to kissing me, his lips taking a delectable walk from my mouth to my neck to my ear.

With no effort at all, Boris sweeps me up, my legs instinctively wrapping around his waist for balance as he walks us over to the chaise. He lowers me down and then stretches me out, kissing me the whole way. When he finally drags his lips off mine, he just stares. Looking a bit dangerous even, his eyes are dark with passion and hunger. I don't have to wonder for long what he has in mind because his hands go to the waistband of my shorts. He raises an eyebrow at me asking permission. So I help him of course. In a matter of moments, I am divested of both my shorts and my panties. Naked from the waist down, and burning up from the fiery heat of his stare.

Then he falls to his knees, as if he's ready to worship me.

"Let me see you."

My whole body must be blushing at his command. I can't breathe and I can't look him in the eye, but I allow my bent knees to part when I feel his hands nudge gently on the inside of my thighs. I'm totally bared to him and one thing's for certain.

He. Is. Looking.

"May I pleasure you, Talia?"

*Yeeeeeeesssss.*

**BORIS**

SHE BLUSHES AN EVEN DEEPER shade of pink but nods slowly several times, her long legs opening up for me even farther in invitation. It's an invitation I don't need to be given twice as I meet her pussy with my mouth. Tongue and lips and teeth explore her swollen wet lips and her sweet pink clit. I suck and lick and bite and tease, taking my cues from her moans of pleasure. Her hips pump against me, her hands pulling my hair. I focus for a long time on her clit, enjoying her sounds before slipping two fingers inside her tight, hot cunt.

She cries out at me. "Yes. Yes. Please. Oh God, yes please!"

I pump my two fingers in and out as I suck on her clit, so swollen with desire. I know she's close and I want her to come. I want her to come on my fingers and my face. I want to taste her as she finds her release.

She's so close. So close. "Let go, *krasotka*," I urge. "Let me feel you come. Will you come for me?"

She moans and juts her hips, riding my face and my fingers, a wild animal. I love it. I finger her so hard, suck on her clit so hard.

"Fuck. Yes!" she screams, and I devour her, letting her ride the wave until she finally slows the movement of her hips.

When she stills, I pull my fingers free from the viselike grip of her orgasm, backing away, wiping my face with the back of my hand. Talia looks at me, eyes heavy-lidded and lustful. Her cheeks are red and there are red splotches along the creamy skin of her neck. I lean forward and kiss each red mark until I find her lips, letting her taste herself on me.

We kiss and kiss, and I feel her hands on my pants, unbuttoning, pulling my cock free. It's so, so hard as she strokes her hand up and down the length. At first, it's slow, leisurely. But the harder our kisses get, the faster her strokes become. She moves her hand only once, to wet it between her own legs before going back to stroking me again. It's such a turn-on. My hands move beneath her shirt, pinching at her hard nipples before pulling her shirt over her head, desperate to finally get a glimpse of the perky tits I remember from our first meeting.

I push the thin, lace bra up on her chest, freeing her breasts, and there they are. Perfect and round and just as perky as I imagined them to be. Her dusky pink nipples are taut with want. I kiss each one, my teeth grazing over her nipples with gentle scrapes. Jutting them into my mouth, I can tell she likes the attention I'm giving them.

The wetness of pre-cum dots the tip of my cock. I'm close, but I don't want to be. Not yet. Talia, however, has other ideas. "I want to see you come," she tells me. "I want to see your face when I make you come. Will you look at me?"

I look up, desperate with need. Wanting her so badly. She's so beautiful with her hair wild from my hands all in it. Her lips swollen from my plundering kisses. Her skin flushed pink from the orgasm I just pulled from her. And as soon as I look into her blue eyes, I'm gone. Lost. Undone.

I come in her hand like a teenager. She strokes me until I'm empty, then falls forward so our foreheads rest against one another. For a long time, we just breathe together.

Suddenly, Talia's shoulders begin to shake, and I'm worried she's crying, embarrassed by our tryst. But when I peer down at her, trying to meet her eyes, I realize she's laughing.

"What is funny?" I ask.

"We're a hot mess," she says, cracking herself up even more. She sits back and gestures between us, her bra around her upper chest, tits out, my cock hanging out of my pants.

I can't help but smile. "We look like two people overcome by passion, I would say."

"You can say that again," she says, practically

wheezing as she tries to get her laughter under control. "Christ on a cracker, this was hot. I think maybe we should rethink the keep-it-professional thing. At least be friends with benefits, right?"

She's so forward. It turns me on. A lot. My cock twitches at thoughts of having her in my bed, spread out, ready to take all of me.

Still, I don't really do casual, and it's what she's suggesting.

"Talia, I don't...I am not really into doing the casual sex thing." Someday I will need to explain to her the reason I feel the way I do, but not tonight, not now.

"It wouldn't be a one-night stand," she says. "And I'm not interested in being with anyone but you."

"So?"

"So, it wouldn't be casual. It would be a consenting, mutually beneficial, exclusive sexual relationship. It's clear we're compatible, and it's clear we both need the release."

"But I do not want you to feel used. That would be the last thing I would want."

"Look, Boris, I trust you. You are good and kind. I would never worry about feeling used when I'm with you. It doesn't have to be serious, but it wouldn't be casual either. We can just enjoy each other and see where it goes."

I stare at her for a good minute before standing to tuck myself back in and zip up. I run a hand through my hair and lean down to kiss her on the forehead. "I want you very badly, Talia. Do not mark my hesitation as a sign of rejection. I just need some time to think about this. Okay?"

She gives me a shy smile. "Okay."

I touch her face one last time before heading out of her apartment, and up to mine.

I don't take a shower this night. Instead, I go to sleep wrapped in her scent, missing her already, considering her words. *It doesn't have to be serious, but it wouldn't be casual either.* But is that enough? If only I can see longer term, do I take this risk?

# 24
# what about the russians?

Talia

I get to my office building, unlocking the mailbox and pulling out a stack of envelopes. There at the top, as has been the same for several days, is a blank white envelope. Inside, I know there will be another magazine-letter threat.

Yesterday, I was told to stop pursuing Boris as a client or have my tits cut off. The day before? Sever all ties with Boris or be gang-raped.

It's been ugly and scary and I'm trying hard to at least act brave, even though I've hardly slept since the night my apartment was ransacked.

Well, other than the nights I slept in Boris's bed.

Today's note says to stop the transfer of funds before it's too late. This one is less creative than the ones before it, but no less effective. When is too late, I wonder?

I call the FBI agent who was assigned to my case after the first break-in and note. He tells me he'll swing by the office to pick it up. I've installed a security system in my office like the one I have at home, and the FBI supposedly has surveillance on both locations now. Still, it doesn't make me feel any safer.

The same internal argument wages war inside me. Do I call and tell Boris about the notes? Do I break ties with him as a client? I've asked Harold for advice and he says to stay the course. If I give in, the bad guys win and all that. Of course, he's told me not to be a hero, not to be stupid. If I sense danger, run. But it seems like madness to take on Russian criminals all on my own, right? It's not like I have friends here in Vegas, or even colleagues. I'm all alone here and I'm risking my life, potentially, for one client.

A client I care about. A client who doesn't deserve to have his hard-earned wealth held hostage, taken by the people charged with investing it for him.

I'll stay the course for Boris's sake—even though I haven't spoken to him since our heavy-duty make-out session last week.

It's been days since we got each other off, since I invited him to be friends with benefits. Days since he kissed me on the forehead and said he would think about it. The same number of nights where I've wished I was in his bed...with him. If only to sleep by his side and feel safe.

I feel like I've been ghosted, and if I'm honest, it's the last thing I expected from Boris.

I stalk the Crush website and social feeds for signs of him, and they are there. There are photos of him at practice, fiercely competitive in his uniform. There are casual photos and Q&As throughout social, with him telling the interviewer about his career to date and his hopes for the Crush this season. With the season about to begin, the hype around this dream team is getting serious. Las Vegas is getting ready to bring the Cup home, and Boris is at the center of those plans.

I'm totally down the rabbit hole on the Crush social feeds when the bells on my office door chime. I nearly jump out of my chair, but it's just Ally.

"Hey there." She smiles brightly. "Sorry to interrupt you. You looked like you were in serious thought."

I close my browser and give her a tight-lipped smile. "No bother at all. What brings you in?"

"Oh, my first paycheck? I think we worked out a weekly schedule, right? And I did the online hours the way you told me."

I shuffle in my seat and try to get my head in the game. "Of course. Yes. Let me take a look."

After pulling up the online form I developed, I see her hours listed and they seem legit, so I send the total over to the little QuickBooks application I set up for Boris and have a check printed.

"So how have things been this first week?" I ask.

"Good," she says, her face brightening. "He's a really sweet guy. We got most of his regular bills set up for ACH debit. We figured it was best since the amounts can fluctuate. We also went through all of his paperwork and got things at least into piles so I can set up files. He wanted a fireproof box for important documents, so we've got one on order. I'll make files once it arrives."

"Sounds like you've been super productive already," I say. What I want to say, but don't is, "Sounds like you spent a lot of time together. Alone."

"We have. I think we'll work on a calendaring system next week, if he doesn't get too distracted by the beginning of the season."

"Hard not to. That's his job."

Ally nods. "I'm so excited to watch him play. I never cared much for sports but knowing an athlete has made me more interested in watching now."

"I'm sure it will be an exciting season." I can barely keep the sarcasm out of my tone.

"He's just such a sweet guy," she says again. "I can't believe he doesn't have a girlfriend or wife."

It's a lot of effort to keep my face neutral when I want to scowl and tell Ally Armstrong to stay the hell away from my man. He's not my man, of course, but he's also not hers. And I'd fight her for him if it really came down to it. She's gushing all over my office and it makes me want to throw up. As it is, I want to toss this woman out on the street and tell her she's fired just for saying he'd be a catch. Christ, am I jealous much, or what? I'm guessing so, as I've never felt this level of antipathy before.

I take a breath and say, "Anything else you need, Ally? I've got a lot of work to do here."

My tone is icy and unwelcoming. I can hear it and Ally sure as hell hears it because her face falls and she just shakes her head. "Sorry to interrupt. Thanks for getting this printed so quickly for me. I'm a poor grad student, so every penny helps."

"Yeah, I'm sorry to be short," I say, realizing what a jealous hag I'm being. "Have a good week, okay?"

She gives a little wave and heads out, and I feel like a total and complete jerk, which is what I am.

I sit, trying to work, for about an hour before I realize how twisted up I am. I need my best friend, so I call Parker.

"Hey, Tallie," she answers on the second ring.

"Hey, Parker," I say, without the usual gusto.

"Uh-oh. I know that tone. That's either the boys-are-dumb or the I-messed-up tone. So which is it?"

"A little bit of both, to be honest."

I tell her every detail. The break-in, my stay at Boris's apartment, the night we jacked each other off. She listens and makes appropriate noises at appropriate times, but when I stop talking she literally says to me, "Talia, stop being such a fucking dumbass."

"Me? I'm being a dumbass?"

"Get your head out of your ass. If you and Boris like each other so much, you should just go for it. You're literally inventing reasons why it can't work, when clearly it could."

"Am not." I pout.

"Just be an adult about it. If he were here, I'd tell him the same thing. You've gone seven days without talking to each other after a hot night of sexy fun times. Because why? He's Mister Moral High Ground and you're Miss Not Making the Same Mistake Twice?"

"That's...I don't even know what to say to all that just now, Parker."

"Well, seriously. You got burned by a married asshole. So what? Tell me, do you like Boris more or less than you liked Cameron?"

"More. Way more."

"And Boris isn't married, right?"

"Right."

"And he's as much as said he wants to date you, and not in a casual way, right?"

"Right."

"So you've got a hot, unmarried professional athlete who wants you and only you and the best you can do is say let's be friends with benefits?"

"It's more complicated than that, Parker. He's my client. My first major new client since moving here. And we've got this weird situation with these Russians—"

"And that man would probably go to the ends of the earth to protect you, let's be honest."

"I mean, I guess..."

"You guess? He let you stay in his apartment. He installed a security system for you. He would, Talia. I know this in my bones."

"So what should I do, then?"

She sighs. "Natalia Wentworth. You are so clueless. Seriously? You call him right this instant and tell him you care about him and want to give it a go.

Like, for real, not some dumbass friends with benefits thing. You want to be his girlfriend."

"Really? I just call him and say I want to be his girlfriend? I mean, why not pass him a note and make him check the yes or no box?"

"Don't be a jerk."

I groan. "I don't know how to do this, Parker. I have next to no experience with men and the first serious thing ended up with me leaving town to avoid the crushing mortification." I will never forget the look in my coworkers' eyes after his wife walked out. I could barely breathe. Could barely see past the well of tears—

"Forget Thompson. Thompson is dead to you. He will never be the poster boy for healthy relationships. So you fell for the wrong guy? It happens to the best of us. But from everything you've said about the Ice Dragon, he's the right guy for you. And you better find a way to not blow it."

"What about the Russians?"

"You leave them to the FBI, but I'm sure the wheel will turn, and it'll all shake out. And bonus, you'll feel safer with two hundred plus pounds of hockey god at your side, regardless."

We talk for a few more minutes and then hang up, a plan forming in my mind.

I TEXT Boris the next night.

Talia: Good luck in the home opener!

He texts me right back. Like, *right* back.

Boris: Good to hear from you.
Thank you.

Talia: I've got my Crush shirt ready.
I'll be there to cheer you on.

Boris: Oh? I'll leave a ticket at Will-
Call for you, then.

Talia: That's sweet, thank you.

Boris: Only the best for my friend and
financial advisor.

Talia: Ouch.

Boris: Sorry. I meant to say I'd love to
take you to dinner tonight. We can
talk. Meet me by the locker rooms
after the game?

Talia: Of course. I'd love to see
you, too.

Boris: I'll make us a dinner
reservation and text you the details.

Talia: Sounds good. Make sure
there's meat on the menu.

Boris: ;-)

I realize after sending that last text that it sounds a bit dirty. But maybe that's okay, considering I have big plans to wear my heart on my sleeve and ravage him completely until he says he'll be my boyfriend. In the back of my mind, I read his texts as a bit cold and worry that he's about to tell me he's done with whatever this is between us, but screw it, I'm going all out, even if I fall on my face.

Two hours later, I'm in a very good box seat with some of the players' wives and significant others. A pretty blonde plops down in the seat beside me, and says, "Who are you?"

It's not a rude question, just a curious one. She's got a broad smile and a big chest.

"I'm, uh, Talia Wentworth?"

"Ohhhh," she says, as if my name means something to her.

"Oh?"

She grins. "You're the one our Boris is all tied up over."

"Oh, he's not...I mean, I'm just his financial advisor."

"His financial advisor and the person he most wants to date," she answers, grinning like a hyena. "We've spent many a therapy session talking about you. I'm Pam, by the way."

"You're his...therapist?" I ask.

"Physical therapist," she answers.

"Oh, okay."

"And how do you feel about him? Just as twisted?"

"Pretty much," I admit.

"Gonna work it out in a big way tonight?"

"I sure hope so," I say.

"Go big or go home. You should look up the story about how I proposed to Georg."

Actually, I read that story. Pamela Jensen arranged a huge pre-game show and proposed to Georg during the playoffs. It was in all the papers, even up in San Francisco. I loved that story. It made me believe in love. I tell her so and she just winks and says, "Welcome to the family. We all fraternize when we're not supposed to around here."

The game starts soon after and I'm instantly into it. It's fast and hard-hitting and the Crush play like a well-oiled machine. Evan Kazmeirowicz scores twice in the first period, just a one-two punch that looks completely effortless. There's the big guy, Viktor, on defense and he just stops everyone like a brick wall as they come toward the goal. The other team can't do a single thing to move the puck forward.

There are two fights, mostly on the defensive side. Boris tries to break them both up, which doesn't surprise me at all. He looks up at the box twice during the game and I wave both times, just to show him I'm really there. I can't wait to see him after the game. I have so much I want to say. So much.

I get really into the game, screaming and yelling a lot. I apologize to my suite-mates, who all tell me yelling is perfectly permissible and this is a safe space. By the third period, I know all their names and they've all given me guidance on how to "go big" when it comes to admitting my feelings for Boris.

In the third period, Boris comes out like a madman and scores two goals, allowing the Crush to win their first game by a hefty four-to-nothing. The arena is a madhouse, it's so loud. Las Vegas came out for the Crush, and their team did not disappoint. I have to say, I think I am a true Crush hockey fan after this game.

I hang in the box for a bit, talking with the women I just met this evening but feel like I've known for a long time, when I get a text from Boris.

> Boris: I forgot about a press event after game.

> Talia: Oh, no big deal.

> Boris: I suck at press so it won't take long. Just meet me at the restaurant so we don't lose our table.

> Talia: Are you doing talk to text?

> Boris: Yes, duh.

> Talia: LOL Okay. See you at the restaurant.

The restaurant is only three blocks away and it's a gorgeous night. The streets are filled with Crush fans, off to celebrate the big win on the Strip. I step out into the night, feeling buoyant and excited and ready to see what this thing with Boris will lead to.

Just a half block from the restaurant, though, I stop dead in my tracks, the hairs on my arms standing straight up when a man steps out of the alley in front of me. I turn to go the other direction, but someone is right behind me. A hand clamps over my mouth before I can scream, and my arms are pulled back so hard I think they may jerk from their sockets.

I try to remember my self-defense classes from college. I stomp down hard on my captor's foot, but he increases his grip as a result. He hisses, "Shut up, bitch," as he pulls me into the dark alleyway. I struggle, trying desperately to get away from him, but his hand is also covering my nose and I can barely breathe. I start to hyperventilate as efforts to escape fade into the sheer terror of trying to catch my breath, trying to stay alert and awake.

I'm dragged and then picked up as if I weigh nothing. There's a moment of weightlessness, then I'm in the back of a van, the metal cold through my T-shirt and jeans. The doors slam and I scream. I scream and scream but as the van starts, no one comes.

## 25

# f#ck the game!

Boris

Sometimes being the boring one on the team pays dividends. Like now. I scored two goals in the game tonight but the press has already figured out that I'm not good for much more than a quick one-sentence soundbite. Tyler is off being his usual obnoxious self, garnering more attention than me, so I'm able to make quick rounds and then slip away, eager to get to Talia at the restaurant.

I make the walk quickly, but when I arrive, Talia is not here. I start to worry maybe she changed her mind. But in my heart, I know she'd tell me if she couldn't make it.

Something feels not right. I know she left ahead of me and she should be here by now.

> Boris: Hey, are you hiding? I'm at the restaurant but I don't see you.

I wait. And wait.

> Boris: Hey, everything okay?

And then the three dots appear. It's a long minute before the reply comes through.

> Talia: We have her. Cancel your contract and leave your money with us or she dies – after we've enjoyed her thoroughly.

> Talia: Such a pretty girl.

My blood runs cold. I put a hand over my mouth to keep from roaring in anger.

I haven't seen red like this since I was a teenager, dyslexic and frustrated and without an outlet. Since before I started playing hockey. Whoever is on the end of the line sends a picture of Talia, bound and gagged, her shirt ripped with a breast exposed. The image makes me think of nothing else other than murder. I will kill these people. Or make them wish they were dead.

With shaking hands, I hit the talk-to-text button and send my reply.

> Boris: What do you want? I'll come. I will give you what you want.

> Talia: Scorpio Street. Look for a rusted metal door. Come alone or she dies.

I run all the way back to the apartment building, first checking Talia's place, which is locked up tight. I head up to my apartment after that, dialing Vlad's number. Go alone? I don't think so. I'm not fucking going alone and I'm sure as hell not letting those guys hurt Talia.

As soon as Vlad answers, I launch into a tirade.

"I asked you to find a way to get me out of this contract. Now they have Talia. You said you'd help me fix this."

"I said these things are always more complicated than we want them to be," Vlad answers. "Good game tonight."

"Good game? I just told you they have Talia and you're telling me good game? Fuck the game and fuck you too!"

"Whoa! I've never heard such language out of you, Boris," Vlad says. "What is this little girl to you anyway? They hit a nerve taking her?"

"Vlad, I swear to God I will ruin you for your business in hockey," I snarl. "They have threatened to kill her. If she is harmed there will be hell to pay so you better send me the best guys you have on the ground in Vegas and send them right fucking now."

"Fine, fine," Vlad says. He chuckles and I swear I would punch him if he were in front of me now. "Hope you marry this one for all the trouble she's causing."

"She is just doing her job, you *debil*. They ordered me to come alone so I need your guys to meet me here at my place first. Now, Vlad. Tell them to come now."

I hang up and head to my closet, pulling a lockbox from the back of the top shelf. In it, a .45 sits, untouched since before I moved to Vegas. I was never into guns much but bought one in Austin so I could learn to shoot. I learned at a range, but it's been a while since I've pulled a trigger.

I load it and put it in my jacket and then wait, pacing for the long minutes until a sharp knock sounds at my door. I swing it open wide, finding three barrel-chested men in dark suits there, each one more menacing than the next. One of them is positively gigantic. He says his name is Huell and that Heisenberg.

Fucking perfect.

I tell them where we're going, and that I'm supposed to go alone.

Huell tells me he knows the place. "There's a way to get in unnoticed. I'll lead my men in from there while you go in the rusty door as expected."

Plan set, we head out on foot. Vlad's men split off two blocks away from the building, disappearing into the shadows as I make myself obvious, staying in the light. I get to the rusted metal door and it swings open, two big men waiting for me. They saw me coming.

I'm patted down, my gun taken away the minute I get in the doorway. I'm led down a dark hallway, through a corridor filled with what I suppose used to be individual offices. Each of the men has a grip on my elbows. They control my movements, our pace. My heart is beating wildly, and the need to see Talia is visceral.

When I do, it takes everything I have to stay neutral and calm.

She's gagged, her arms and legs tied tightly to the chair she sits on. Her shirt is torn, her breast still exposed to all who want to look. She's got a bruise blooming on her right cheek and blood trickles from her bottom lip.

"You're as good as dead," I say under my breath. "I will rip your limbs off."

I'm shoved to the ground, a knee in my back. One of them grabs me by the hair and kicks me in the stomach, enough to take the wind out of me. The other steps away, pulling his cock out. He shakes it at Talia, taunting her, telling her how much she'll like having it up her ass. She winces and closes her eyes as I try to stand. Suddenly, there is a third man in the room, and two of them are holding me back as the guy with his cock out strokes himself, pushing his limp prick toward Talia's mouth. She's gagged, so there isn't much he'd be able to do anyway, but the kidnappers all laugh. They say, in Russian, for him to spread her apart and take her. To teach me a lesson.

They don't know it yet, but they just signed their death warrants.

At the end of this night, the world will be less a few of its degenerate scum, because these motherfuckers are going to die.

TALIA

SEEING Boris rage against his captors is absolutely terrifying, and yet he fills me with hope. He came for me. I shouldn't be surprised because he has always shown his protective side, but watching him transform into an enraged Incredible Hulk on a mission for justice is something altogether spellbinding to witness.

As soon as the one guy whipped out his cock and started waving it in my face, Boris became supercharged. Their exchange in Russian, I didn't understand of course, but whatever they said wound Boris up to the point he managed to break free, throwing punches left and right, as well as taking some in return. He's not a fighter, but he is a hockey player so he's not unskilled in defending himself. He body-checks one guy into the cement wall, smashing his head hard enough to make him wobbly. That guy falls to the floor as a second one swings at Boris, hitting him in the side of the head. Boris appears stunned for a moment but manages to stay on his feet.

*Bang! Bang!*

Gunshots ring out as two of our captors fall from direct shots to the head, blood pooling around them on the floor. There's no way they can still be alive. I'm in shock at what I'm seeing—a gun battle right in front of me—and hearing, as people shout and scream and bleed out. Boris rushes me as the men continue to take shots at each other, taking me to the ground with him while untying the ropes binding me to the chair.

He works quickly, telling me he's going to get me out, shielding me from a position on the floor where we are more protected. The second I'm free from the ropes, he drags me up and out into the hallway, pocketing a lone gun left on the side counter along the way. I can't resist kicking the guy who swung his dick at me, as hard as I can in the nuts, when we pass by him crying on the floor like a baby.

A huge black man speaks to Boris. "Leave it to us. We'll make sure the message is clearly relayed."

We don't need to be told twice. Boris covers me with his jacket and rushes us out of the room, back through the maze of offices, and out into the warm Las Vegas night.

We're two blocks away when we hear the screaming of police sirens.

# 26
# krasotka

Talia

It hurts to open my eyes. I think I may just lie here with my eyes closed for the rest of my life.

Everything hurts, feels swollen, or aches. Swallowing is an effort. I force my eyes to open, but one doesn't want to open all the way. My right eye. An area above my right cheekbone stings with tenderness.

It takes a great effort to sit up, and to look around, and then to realize I'm in Boris's bed at his apartment. I don't even remember coming here. The last thing I can remember about last night is fleeing from the nightmare of the evil dudes who kidnapped me, being taken out by some possibly less-evil dudes in a shootout, and then running down a dark street hand in hand with Boris to the sounds of screaming police sirens. I must have passed out somewhere along the way.

My hand shifts into a warm body and I stiffen. Turning my head ever so slowly, I see Boris lying next to me, on top of the covers, shirtless, his hair askew on the pillow, his mouth parted slightly.

I try to reach out to touch him, but it hurts. It hurts so much. When I moan involuntarily his eyes snap open immediately.

"You okay?" he asks quietly.

"Just hurts," I manage, sounding very garbled.

"Oh, *krasotka*." He orders me to drink some water and then forces two huge tablets of extra-strength Ibuprofen down me that have to be swallowed one at a time. When that's done, he helps me to lie back down into his soft bed once more. When I fall asleep a second time, it's to him massaging my scalp and trailing his fingers through my hair, soothing me with soft touches and comforting me with sweet words.

*Whispering to me in Russian.*

I don't know what the words mean, only how they make me feel.

Cherished and safe and precious.

**THE SECOND TIME I AWAKEN,** I feel so much better it's downright miraculous.

Boris is still by my side in the bed, looking as anxious and intense as before though.

"You're awake, *krasotka*. How are you?" He presses a kiss to my forehead.

"I feel a million times better than before," I assure him.

"Did they...hurt—"

"No. Just smacked me around a little. Nothing major."

He lets out a laugh but it's bitter, angry, and slightly terrifying.

"They're either dead or in police custody by now, and I'm here safe with you."

"Thank God," he says before pressing another kiss to my head, against my hair this time.

"No, thank *you*, Boris." I cough, but then I groan because the coughing makes it hurt more.

"Get some more rest, *krasotka*. No need to rush anything right now."

"Need to pee," I say.

"Okay," he says, rolling away, his feet hitting the floor. He helps me to my feet, then walks me to the bathroom. I stare at him until he gets the message that I can do this small thing by myself. But instead of closing the door, he just turns his back. I don't know if he thinks bad guys are going to crawl out of the toilet to get me or what, but he's clearly not letting me too far out of his sight for the moment.

His phone rings, shrill and hurting my head. He answers in Russian, speaks in Russian. When he hangs up, he says, "All accounts have been transferred. They will not be bothering us again."

I finish up and wash my hands, then splash some water on my face and try not to look at my reflection in the mirror. It's not a pretty sight but the cool water feels refreshing and cleansing after my ordeal.

Boris leads me back to bed.

"Thank you." My voice sounds scratchy. "For coming for me."

"Why would you thank me? I got you into this mess."

"You got me out of it. You came for me."

"But I would have gone to the ends of the earth to get you," he whispers, his chocolaty eyes boring into me. "I'm so sorry, *krasotka*. So, so sorry."

"I had this whole big speech planned." I swallow and wince. "But right now—"

"Save it," he interrupts. "There will be another time. Another day. Just rest now, *krasotka*."

Another day, indeed.

As I start to drift away with Boris warm and protective at my side, I'm really curious to know the translation for *krasotka*. "What does it mean?" I ask sleepily.

"Gorgeous beauty."

I'm pretty sure I'm smiling as I fall asleep.

THE NEXT TIME I WAKE, I'm still sore, but more aware of my surroundings. I drag on my glasses from the side table and peer at my phone. While I've certainly lost track of time, I think I've been sleeping for like two whole days.

My mouth feels as dry as a cotton ball and I have crazy bad breath. Boris is not in the bed to micromanage me, so I get up and shuffle to the bathroom, turning on the shower as I brush my teeth using my index finger and some of Boris's toothpaste. There's an ugly bruise on my cheek, my lip is slightly puffy, and my hands are pretty scratched up. All in all, it could be worse. Way worse.

I pull off the T-shirt Boris must have put me into —an extra-large Austin Comets tee—and then shimmy out of my panties. When I step under the hot water, it stings at my bruises and scratches but it's more comfort and relief than anything.

I take my time, closing my eyes as I tilt my head back to wet my hair. It feels exquisite to get clean and wash away the filth of that night. I wasn't sure when or how I'd wash away the fear and terror of the night...

When I open my eyes, Boris is at the door to the bathroom. The shower glass is clear, and he can see all of me. I stand, hands at my sides, making no effort whatsoever to cover myself.

Boris steps forward, pulling his white T-shirt over his head before exposing powerful thighs and a fully aroused, very beautiful penis when he drops his shorts. He hesitates at the threshold of the shower, waiting for permission. I nod, and he steps under the steamy spray with me. It's a snug fit for two people, especially when one is as big as he is. He's close and his closeness makes me forget my aches and pains. All I feel is desire.

He reaches out and strokes the bruise on my cheek just ever so lightly.

"It will fade." I remind him that he was hurt too

when I kiss the ugly bruises on his ribs and on his side.

Boris nods and swallows back whatever he thought to say. His thumb moves to rub against my swollen bottom lip before he leans in, kissing me, a feather soft thing that does nothing to tame the heat pooling between my legs.

"You said you had a big speech for the restaurant," he says, taking the soap and washing my shoulders and arms.

"I did," I answer, smiling up at him. "Basically, I was going to tell you that I care for you a whole lot and I think we should be together. I mean, I was going to be way more romantic about it, but in light of everything that's happened..."

He grins. "Do you feel that way still?"

"Definitely."

"Good." He smiles. "So, tell me."

"Tell you?" Big strong hands lather the soap gently over my breasts as I close my eyes, sighing with simple pleasure.

"Tell me what you were going to say. I don't think it is too late."

His hands roam, fingertips playing at my pebbled nipples, trailing down my slick and soapy stomach. I can hardly think about anything else, let alone all the things I had planned to say the other night.

"I was..." I moan as he fits two fingers inside of me. "I was going to say that I really like you. That I....ahhhh..."

His fingers pump in and out of me, deliciously

unhurried. It feels sinfully good, and makes me forget that my face is bruised and my lip is swollen. "Is this okay?" he asks, as if my moans of pleasure aren't enough evidence of consent.

"Yes," I whisper. "Yes, it's wonderful. And I think you're amazing. Honestly? You're the best man I've ever met. And I'm done pretending I don't want you, or that I can live without you, because neither of those things are true."

Boris's free hand rubs along the length of my spine, down to my rear, cupping one ass cheek, pulling me closer. His erection pushes against my stomach. "I'm glad to hear all of those things."

"Yeah?" I ask, my lips skimming his chest.

"Oh yeah. Because I feel the same. When I found out you'd been taken—Talia, I am not a violent man, but I was ready to kill anyone standing in my way to protect you."

I don't know what to say, so I just reach around, splaying my hands against his broad, strong back. My fingertips dig into the hard planes of muscle as I press fully against him, skin to skin. His fingers leave my body but he brings me in even tighter into him, our bodies aligned as we embrace under the steaming water.

"I think I'm in love with you," he says in my ear.

It's much too soon, right? Too soon for him to say things like that to me. But my heart is thundering in my ears as I look up, meeting his intense gaze, and I can see that he means it. I can see the emotion in his eyes. And when he kisses me, it's soft and careful, passionate and protective.

"I feel deeply connected to you, I have for a while now. I tried to keep it professional, but I think this might be the real deal between us. I want to try to make something of it."

"So do I, *krasotka*."

*Gorgeous beauty.* That Boris thinks of me as a gorgeous beauty is probably my biggest surprise of all, but I'll never complain about it.

He turns off the shower and wraps me in a big, fluffy towel before taking one for himself. After I'm dry, he leads me to the bed, pressing me back onto fresh sheets and peeling away my towel.

Baring my body so I'm naked, there's nothing but hot fevered skin between the two of us aching for the other's touch.

I sink back onto soft pillows and wait for him to join me.

He asks if I want him to wear a condom, saying he will go out and get some if I need him to.

I shake my head no and tell him there's no need because I get a birth control shot every three months, and that I trust him.

Also that I will die if he leaves me hanging right now to go condom shopping.

He laughs darkly and drops the towel.

BORIS SPENDS a long time kissing every inch of my body. He rubs and massages my aching muscles as he goes, sending me into some blissful place between relaxation and combustion. He kisses and licks at my breasts, telling me how beautiful I am, how amazing my body is. He teases me as his lips and tongue move against the inside of my thighs, his shoulders forcing me to open my legs wide and bare myself to him.

It's only minutes before I'm coming, his tongue sinister and talented against my clit. His grin is pure bad boy when he emerges victorious, moving up to kiss along my neck and jaw, careful of my injuries. I want him in me so badly that I'm desperately impatient, so when he turns onto his back, I climb on top, straddling his hips and aligning his cock to my entrance. He watches his cock disappear inside me as I sink down onto his whole hard length, both of us moaning in pure pleasure. Our bodies fit perfectly together...and nothing has ever felt so right.

His hands are cupping both cheeks of my ass as we start to move together. I'm so full with his cock deep inside of me. I feel claimed and complete, like this is what I was always supposed to feel but never knew. Nonsensical noises escape my throat as I ride him. It takes no time before I'm coming and clenching around his cock, the orgasm hitting me sharply when he sits up and starts nipping at my breasts and nipples with his teeth. The hint of delicious pain sending me over the edge all in an instant.

We're all wrapped up in each other, so close,

moving together, breathing together, hearts pounding, kissing, tasting, fucking together.

Boris twists me to my back without ever separating his body from mine.

"I need to look in your eyes when I take you, *krasotka*."

And so he does.

We stay locked on each other as he moves, pumping his cock in long, deep slides in and out of me, his pace ever increasing. It's a beautiful torture as I build again. Up, up, up I go until he kisses me fiercely and his cock becomes impossibly harder, spasming as he comes inside me. I fall into another sweeter climax, pausing from breathing as the sharp sting of pain-laced ecstasy overtakes my whole body in a tingling, hot rush.

Boris puts his forehead against mine as he finishes. He looks meditative, as if his experience was as life-altering as mine was.

I'm in awe of this connection we have, this chemistry. I can't find words to say it, but I know this is right. It's meant to be. I don't ever want it to go away.

I TRACE the dragon tattoo with my finger along the intricate inked design from his shoulder to his forearm. Green blends into turquoise, which blends to blue, which blends to purple, and into black. It's a stunning work of Asian art, striking in form and context. With one deviation. Instead of the more typical red ball incorporated into the design, there's a flat black disc. A hockey puck. His dragon is not a mean-looking one. Boris's dragon is brave and honorable, just like the man.

My man.

I can say it now. *My man.* Because he is mine, and I am his.

We've been lying together in the bed, naked and sated, for a long time, dozing off here and there, sharing sweet kisses, caressing each other's skin, when the ring of his doorbell invades our peace.

Boris sits up and peers at his phone before exiting the bed, pulling on a pair of jeans lying nearby on the floor.

He disappears, shutting the bedroom door behind him.

I force myself from the bed and zip into the bathroom to retrieve the Comets T-shirt and Boris's discarded athletic shorts where he dropped them in front of the shower. The black shorts are positively huge on me, but at least they have a drawstring that I can cinch up tight enough to stay on my hips. I pull my hair up in a messy bun and pad out to the living room, only to find Ally reviewing something with Boris at the kitchen island.

Ally hands me a cup of coffee from my favorite nearby coffee shop. It's fresh and hot and tastes like heaven. "Thank you, Ally. How did you know?"

"A little birdie sent a text and told me you might

be having caffeine withdrawal. You doing okay? I heard you took a nasty fall."

I look at Boris and realize he's not spreading the news of my abduction widely. Thankfully. I nod and say, "Yeah. I'm such a super klutz. That's what I get for reading books instead of doing sports all my life."

"Boris," Ally interrupts, "you've got a team meeting in half an hour, then you've got to get back and pack for your preseason road trip."

"Thanks. And thanks for the information on that class."

"I'll walk you to the arena so we can go over the week's schedule," Ally says, heading toward the door.

Boris disappears into his closet, returning in shorts and T-shirt. He shoves his feet into his trainers and throws his workout bag over his shoulder, then makes his way over to me.

"Stay as long as you need, *krasotka*. I should be back in a couple of hours and I will find you."

He kisses me on top of the head before meeting Ally at the door. The young woman watches our exchange with interest but keeps any feelings carefully masked. She says goodbye to me as they leave. I give a little wave in return as the door shuts, not sure I know how to read Ally yet. She must be crushing on Boris, because how could she not. But she was professional and invested...that's good, right?

There's no reason to hang around here for two hours, so I find my phone, keys, and the fanny pack I was wearing on game day, and head down to my own apartment. LuLu meows like she's been left alone for a year as I shut myself inside. I pick her up, rubbing her soft fur and missing her sweetness as she purrs. I know Boris has been taking care of her here because he told me so.

I'm so tired. From the ordeal. From the lovemaking. From the intense emotions. I lie down on the chaise with my favorite blanket, LuLu making herself comfortable wedged between my side and the edge of the chaise.

I drift away wondering just one thing…

Should I have told Boris that I might love him, too?

# 27
# naked storytime

Boris

Ally rattles off the schedule for the week. I'll pack tonight for a short flight to Anaheim tomorrow morning. We'll condition, do a press event, and then chill for a bit before our first game. We then travel to Los Angeles for game two on the road. We'll finish two nights later in Portland. I'll be gone for four days and it feels like forever, knowing Talia will be left here alone. I approached Viktor at practice yesterday and asked if he could point me in the right direction for hiring private security to watch over Talia when she goes to and from her office. He told me to call the same guy Vlad mentioned, Saul Heisenberg, local fixer of all problems—for a price. I told Viktor price is nothing to me compared to peace of mind for the safety of my *krasotka*. He slapped me on the back and typed Heisenberg's number into my phone himself. I considered our fences mended.

"Do you want to try for the Saturday morning session?" Ally is asking.

I give her an apologetically quizzical look.

"The dyslexia session?" she asks.

"It sounds really awful, Ally."

"It's a mix of cognitive stimulation and introduction to some cheat tools they've developed," she says. "It's up to you."

"I'll think about it." And I will. "But thank you for doing the research."

We're nearly to the arena. I thank Ally again and tell her I really appreciate her assistance with my schedule. She nods and starts to walk away before turning back. "Boris?"

"Yes?"

"Things are different between you and Talia now, aren't they?"

"They are." I gave her an answer, but I don't feel like I owe her more than that.

She nods again, a small smile playing on her lips. "All good. I could see it coming a million miles away. Talk to you once you get on the road."

"YOU GUYS WERE A MACHINE OUT THERE," Coach is saying. "Bring that same energy and organization on the road and I can't see us doing anything but heading to the playoffs by season's end. We have to keep the momentum going. We have to *play with purpose*—every single game."

Our owner and GM are both here, too, and they've

given us the same pep talk. Coach's came with a few notes first, of course. The reality is that these first few games are all pre-season. What will really matter is our true home opener in two weeks. We have to win there in order to keep the momentum going into our long season.

We finish up the meeting and a few of us head to the gym to get a light workout in. I follow mine with a trip to the physical therapy rooms. My shoulder's a mess again, so Pam has me hop up on the table so she can dig into the muscle.

"Wow, what did you do, get in a fight?" she asks jokingly.

I just grunt a response because that's exactly how I jacked it up again. Clearly, telling her I had to enlist a group of shady dudes from Vegas to rescue the woman I love from another group of shady fuckers from Russia is not happening.

"Not talking today?" Pam asks. "Fine. I'll do the talking. I met your lady at the game the other night. Talia Wentworth, big-glasses-wearing financial genius. She hit it off with the First Wives Club right away, so they know about her now. She's no longer your secret dream girl anymore. Still just friends, are we? Oh…sorry, *professional colleagues*?"

I snort at this because her tone is so ridiculous. "You're nosy."

"You started it by pouring your guts out and asking for advice. Plus, we're family. You and Georg are blood relations. I'm your cousin now, too." She pokes my shoulder a little over hard to get her point across. "Family shares shit about their lives with each other. So, spill. How did she go with the grand gesture? Did she go big?"

*I would say being kidnapped and nearly raped going a little too big ...*

"Okay. Yes. We had a breakthrough and are on the same page. Happy?"

"Very. Good for you, Boris." She sticks her tongue out at me.

I leave with a stupid grin on my face.

**I BROUGHT** Talia to my place on the guise of helping me pack for my road trip, but I have a few other plans for us tonight in addition to the packing. I just got her, and now I must leave her behind and here alone while she's still healing from what they did to her in the abduction? It's fucked-up and I hate it very much.

She's in my closet right now choosing shirts and ties to go with the two suits I'm taking on said trip I don't want to take.

"What do you think of this green tie to go with the windowpane check and this blue shirt?" She's sexy as fuck with her legs for days in gray shorts, and a tiny pink top with no bra; standing at the threshold of my closet, my clothes in her hands, (which she chose for me) asking for my opinion.

A dark shadow of a bruise is visible on her cheek and her hands still show the many scratches and cuts, but her beauty is not diminished even in the slightest.

Not to me.

I stalk over to her, take the hanger with the shirt from her hand and toss it on my bed.

"I really like the green tie for the blue shirt," she chatters, "but what do you think?"

I take the green tie from her and loop it behind her neck, tugging her against me. "I think I like it best when you are wearing it, *krasotka*."

"Oh yeah?" she says with a smirk. "Maybe the tie and nothing else, probably?" she teases.

"I won't say no to that, but I was thinking more about sneaking you along with me for this road trip. I don't like leaving you alone so soon after—"

"I will be fine right here with LuLu and my books." She shakes her head at me, not entertaining any discussion on the matter. "I'll be watching every game and we can even FaceTime after if you want to." She wiggles her eyebrows at me suggestively. "That could be fun. But at the end of the day, you have a job to do and so do I."

I groan in frustration because even though I don't like it, I know she's right. I have to help the Crush win hockey games on the road, and she has to help people manage their money here in Vegas. "Okay, so the sooner we get me packed, the sooner I can take you to bed and have you read some more from the Iain Cooper book."

"Whoa there, dragon man. You're taking me to bed to have me *read* to you?" She wrinkles her nose at me, unable to hide her disappointment.

"Oh yeah. It will be days and days before you can read to me again, so I want to make the most of our night here together."

"Umm, okay, if that's what you want to do...I guess I can read to you." She doesn't look convinced but she's trying her best to be. She's adorable.

"I do have one request though, if you don't mind."

"Yes? What would that be?" Her eyes flash up at me curiously.

"You're going to be naked while you read to me—well, you may wear this green tie if you like, but that is all."

MANY HOURS AND ORGASMS LATER, when I have her warm and naked beside me in my bed, I know that Talia is set apart from all other women I have ever known in my life. She's this nerdy math and money girl who can be bold and shy at the same time. She loves books and eats meat like it's going out of style. She's always got something spilled on her clothes. She's got a mouth worse than my teammates, sometimes. She's strong and bold and sexually unafraid. Talia Wentworth is amazing. And I am in love with her. I'm sure of it.

But I also know I have to be content with just this for now, because she's not ready for more than this. To hold her, to share my bed with her, to hear her breathing as she falls asleep, that will have to be enough…for now.

OUR FIRST GAME on the road at Anaheim is a win. I score one goal to Evan's two. He's playing the best I've ever seen him this season, and that's saying something because he is a legend. I've heard rumors he might retire in the next season or two. He's still young, but he has two kids now, a wife. He's talked about coaching somewhere. I think he's ready to change the pace of his life.

We go for a beer after the game and when I ask him about it, he gives a vague shrug.

"My wife would like me home more, I'm sure, but I'll always love playing the game. Coaching would still require a lot of traveling, so maybe broadcasting might be more of a future goal. I still have time to think about it, but the wheel keeps on turning, you know? Not getting any younger."

"I wondered. I just started seeing someone and I feel bad leaving her behind already."

Evan's eyebrows shoot into his hairline. "You're dating someone? Really?"

"Is it so hard to believe?"

"No, I mean, I guess…never mind. Who is she?"

"My investment manager," I say with a chuckle. "Talia."

"Wow, she's some investment manager."

"She's a genius when it comes to managing my 'puck-money' as she calls it. She's smarter than me by a mile."

He smiles. "Those are the really special ones. Good for you, man. I hope it works out."

I HAVE a hard time sleeping after the Anaheim game. Thoughts of what could've happened to Talia the night she was kidnapped creep into my headspace at odd times. It's too much to stomach when I delve too deeply down the rabbit hole of what-ifs and *why nots*.

My mind is not in the game when we lose to Los Angeles. I admit, I do not play my best, and I hear it from Coach after the game. Back at the hotel in a funk, I decide to call Talia.

"How are things in Sin City?" I ask.

"Same as before you left. How are things in the City of Angels? Did you know you're in my hometown?"

"Ahh, yes, I do remember you saying your family was in LA. Maybe I would have played better tonight if you were here in the stands. I think you are my good luck charm, *krasotka*."

"You didn't become the Ice Dragon because of one game, Boris," she says. "You earned that name. You earned your reputation. One shitty game does not make or break your career. It's just the preseason and my being there or not has zero to do with the talent and ability you've been honing since you were a kid. Your success is not dependent on me, though I'm certainly always rooting for you."

"How did you get so wise at such a young age?" I ask.

"Kid genius, remember?"

"Right, I forgot you went to college at, like, twelve. I was getting kicked out of school for fighting at twelve."

"And yet here you are, one of the NHL's top scorers. And one of its best-known pacifists."

"I wasn't such a pacifist when—"

"No," she says. "I don't want to talk about it."

"But are you okay about it?" I ask, hoping she might tell me that much at least.

"I don't think I'm suffering any significant emotional trauma over it, if that's what you're asking."

I'm quiet for a moment. "You're the strongest person I think I've ever met."

"I'm not," she says. "There are so many people out there fighting much more serious battles. Was I scared? Yes. Did I think there was a real chance I might not make it out of there? Yes. But I did, and you were there to save me. You gave me the number for the private security to call if I ever feel scared. That's enough for right now. I am so appreciative of you trying to help me to feel safe again, but now things are quiet and fine. *I'm* fine."

"I think you are, *krasotka*."

But I have to fight to convince myself to believe it.

WE WIN our final game in Portland by a large margin, three of the goals being mine. It's my first hatty with the Crush, and even though preseason numbers don't count for career stats, it's my sixth. So, overall a good result, a game more like our first one against Anaheim. I feel the team is gelling once more after a short slump. I can't wait to get back to my Talia though. There's so much I want to tell her. We still need to talk about so many things. I know next to nothing about her family and her life before she came to Las Vegas. Likewise, with me. I've not shared much at all about my past growing up, and she deserves to know all of it.

After we land in Vegas the next afternoon, I unload from the baggage claim, shoulder my bag, and take an Uber straight to Talia's office. I make one stop for a bouquet of pale pink roses, then take the flight of stairs up one floor, bursting into her office with the energy of a child on Christmas morning.

She's on the phone, but her eyes light up when she sees me, a wry grin pulling one side of her mouth up. She's talking to a client about his quarterly results and I know I should be a gentleman, let her finish her call. But I simply can't do it.

I step behind her desk and kiss her neck. She ignores me, mostly, which only emboldens me more. I want her. I want her attention. I want her body.

My mouth works against her creamy skin and I'm pleased to see her nipples pucker against the thin fabric of her blouse. I feel her up from outside her shirt and she leans her head back, clearing her throat as she tries to finish her conversation.

The moment she hangs up the phone, I've got her up and splayed across her desk, which is risky if a client walks in. But I don't care if someone sees us. I am simply overcome by lust. Pure lust because I've had her now and I won't let her go. Filthy thoughts run through my head as I pluck open the buttons of her blouse, baring her sweet, creamy breasts encased in a lacy white bra.

*Mine.*

It's not like me to feel this territorial. But then again, I've always said I don't do casual. This is real for me. It's the real thing—she is mine and I am hers. The need to brand her right here in this nearly public space is a wild notion made real when she responds with a growl, tearing at my zipper and pulling my cock from my pants. In seconds I'm beneath her skirt, pushing her panties to the side, burying my cock into her wet, warm depths.

*Oh, fuck!*

*YA khochu trakhnut' tebya navsegda!* I shout a string of Russian curses before pressing a blistering kiss to her lips. She bites my bottom lip as I pick up the pace, fucking in and out of her, the need to come inside and mark her as mine, a running mantra in my head.

When I feel her cunt clamping down on my cock, and know she's coming, I allow myself to follow her over the edge. It's hot and intense and explosive as I come hard, pounding into her until my cock is wrung dry. *What the fuck was that? And when the hell can I do that again?*

After one luxurious moment of kissing her, I'm reminded that we've just fucked on her desk, at her place of business, in the middle of her workday. Anyone could come in the door at any moment and discover us. Guiltily I pull her to her feet so we can crowd into the little office bathroom to clean up.

"Well, hello to you, too," she says, blushing heavily.

"Sorry, that was—I don't know what that just was."

"Intense?"

"I couldn't wait," I say with a shrug.

"Guess not. But thank you. It's good to be wanted."

"You are. Wanted. Always."

She smooths her hair and checks her blouse before walking back out to her desk. I follow her out, feeling her mood change and a chill descend over us.

"Everything okay?" I'm not imagining it, am I? "I'm sorry, *krasotka*, I was so...desperate with you."

She gives me a sad smile. "I'm fine. It felt good. It's just...maybe this is going too fast?"

Shock strikes me with a painful blow to the heart. "I'm sorry?"

"It's just...something you said on the road about me being your lucky charm? I'm not, Boris. I can't be. You built your brand long before you met me. And I don't know if I'm ready to be part of the wives' club or whatever. This is...it's an intense feeling between us. I feel it. It's real. But I need…I think we both need to take a breather. Slow it down."

"I don't think I know what you are asking for."

"I know you're not a casual relationship guy, you're all in or you're not in at all. I get that. But this is…it's really intense, really fast, you know? What happened to dating?"

"We can," I say. "I'll take you on a million dates."

"I just…I think maybe we need some space."

"I do not need space," I tell her. "But if you do, then I'll respect your wishes."

"Thank you." Her voice doesn't sound the same as she sits in her office chair and flicks her hair back behind her shoulders. I see the very moment she switches to professional mode, though, her back going ramrod straight, her lips pursing in concentration.

"I've got all of your investments set up. Early indicators look good, but the market is somewhat volatile due to the upcoming election, so there's some fluctuation. Your first quarterly earnings report will be ready in October, but the January report will be more telling. We can make adjustments as needed at that point."

I feel myself backing away, horrified, shocked, angry. What the hell is going on here? I left the airport and rushed over here to see the woman I love. We had sex on her desk. She came. I came. And now she's behaving like I'm a fucking client, in full professional mode.

I feel sick about whatever she's doing here. But if

she wants space, I have to give it to her. I don't have a choice.

I'm in a daze as I leave her office. It's good my subconscious knows the way home, because I don't think I could consciously make my way there right now. Over and over I replay how I burst into her office, so eager to see her, to have her. I was a brute. I took her like some animal, rutting into her with no self-control. I scared her away and it's my fault. I did this. *But there are two people in a relationship.* And perhaps right now, because I called her my lucky charm, she's not actually as committed as I thought. And there is fucking nothing I can do about that. *Shit.*

BRUCE, my dyslexia coach, is a nice guy but he tries too hard to be funny. My first session is completed, and even though I am most decidedly not in a funny mood, I can see the value, so I make another appointment for the following week.

Ally meets me at the Starbucks across the street after my session so we can go over the next week's schedule. There's a lot of internal Crush stuff happening on the calendar this month. Social media, photo shoots, and press events to gear up for the big home opener. We review and get everything calendared into my phone, but as we finish up, she's onto me. I'm not fooling anyone.

"Boris, will you tell me what's up with you, please?"

"Talia broke things off," I admit.

"Why on earth would she do that?"

"She just said things were moving too fast. She needed space."

"Space to continue to act like she isn't in love with you?"

"She's not in love with me," I say. "But I thought she might get there someday."

"How long have you guys known each other?"

"Only a few months. And we had a rather serious experience not long ago. I think it scared her a lot more than she's admitting."

"The thing where she fell?" Ally asks in a knowing tone.

"She didn't fall. She was abducted and held hostage. I had to break her out."

"Whoa."

"It was intense. Scary. I would have been scared if I was her, and it was my fault. The guys were after my money and they used her as bait."

"That's insane. And she's pretty young, right?"

"Early twenties. She said she hasn't really had a relationship before."

"I think there's a lot to unpack. But if it's real, you'll find a way. You have to earn trust. Relationships and trust take time to build, Boris. My advice? Give Talia the space she's asking for but also make sure she knows how you feel about her."

"So, you think I should fight for her, then?"

"I mean, it sounds like you already have. Like, literally." Ally grins. "But hell yeah."

I have some work to do. Actually, a great deal of work.

And maybe I'm more of a fighter than I thought.

Fight? For Talia, my beloved *krasotka*, puck-money goddess?

Hell yes, I will fight.

# 28
# quidditch match?

Talia

" I don't think I'm going," I say, arms folded with feet firmly planted.

"Don't be a baby," Parker says. "You said yourself you loved the first game."

"And then I got kidnapped and slapped around by a bunch of goons." I lift my chin at her and stand my ground.

But Parker gets up in my face, and then she pulls me into an awkward hug, my still-folded arms wedged between us. "I know you keep saying you're fine, but I don't think you're really fine, are you?"

I bury my head in my best friend's shoulder and cry. It's the first time I've allowed myself to break down. I've tried to convince myself I was fine, but she's right; I'm not fine. She doesn't ask me to talk about it. She knows what happened. She knows I'm having horrific nightmares and waking up terrified. She knows Boris saved me. She knows I pushed him away. There's no need to rehash it.

Parker just lets me cry for a very long time. Finally, when the tears subside, I pull away.

"I probably look like a blotchy, red mess," I say, sniffling.

"You do, but it's okay. You needed that, huh?"

"I think I really did." I wipe under my eyes to get the last remnants of tears brushed away.

She sighs. And that's the thing with Parker. She will rip into me when I'm being a dumbass, but she'll also come to my rescue to stand by my side. *Literally.* And when she sighs like this, I hear her unspoken promise. *You will get through this, and I'm by your side until you do.* God, I'm thankful for her.

"Talia, we can't live our lives in fear, can we?" No. She's right about that. "Let's get dressed up and go see a Crush home opener."

We certainly can. There are two tickets at Will-Call with my name on them waiting to be claimed. Because Boris has made sure to send me messages and gifts daily since our breakup a little over a week ago. The first delivery was a dozen dark pink roses with a handwritten note that said:

> *Krasotka,*
>
> *Dark pink roses stand for "appreciation and gratitude" both of which I feel for you. I will be forever grateful I walked into your office that day and found the best puck-money goddess in the world. I miss you.*
>
> *Boris*

His handwriting isn't the prettiest, but I can tell he has labored over his message, because it's perfect with no mistakes in the spelling or otherwise. Every day since, a different color of roses has arrived along with a handwritten note in the same disorderly scrawl.

The second delivery was a dozen pure white roses plus a one-year subscription to MeowBox for LuLu. A box of gourmet cat treats and kitty-friendly toys will be delivered each month to LuLu Wentworth, tailored specifically for her. His note though? Even more touching than the gift.

> *Krasotka,*
>
> *Two meanings for white roses are "purity and heavenly." My feelings for you are as "pure" as they come and it feels like "heaven" being with you, so the color white is very fitting I think. But white also reminds me of your sweet LuLu, who I am also missing very much.*
> *Boris*

The third delivery contained two dozen red-tipped yellow roses and a fancy subscription box from The Bookworm Box—romance themed—the biggest one they have, of course. The proceeds from the subscription boxes go to charity, so I know he's spent a great deal of money. I can now look forward to special editions signed by my favorite authors to add to my collection each month, but it was his sweet note that made me cry all the tears.

> *Krasotka,*
>
> *Yellow roses tipped with red mean "friendship and falling in love." We started out as friends and I liked you right away. I knew you were smart and kind and beautiful, but the night you first read to me was when I started to fall in love with you. I miss you reading to me almost as much as I miss you. Almost...*
>
> *Boris*

Day after day it went on with roses and presents and letters. I've sent a thank-you text for each gift with a picture of the accompanying roses, so he'd know I'd received them. Even if I haven't been ready to see him quite yet, I wanted him to know the romantic gifts and his heartfelt notes were accepted and read by me. But otherwise, we haven't spoken. My apartment and office are swimming in the scent of roses, and both could pass for florist's shops. I have more subscriptions and gift cards than I know what to do with. The Designer Eyes gift certificate in an obscene amount of money for custom Tiffany & Co frames probably takes the cake for most impressive, though. It's a straight-up fact Boris Drăghici has game when it comes to romancing a woman. Undisputed fact.

Each arrangement of roses and gifts has been more impressive than the last. Right up to the one that arrived earlier today. A gorgeous display of easily three dozen red roses with a large box and a note.

*Krasotka,*

*A red rose can have many meanings—Love, Passion, Beauty, Courage—among them. I know you are beautiful both inside and out or I wouldn't call you 'krasotka' all the time. It is simply how I think of you, and I cannot change how I feel. I witnessed your courage in the face of terror and saw your warrior heart in action. Talia Wentworth, you are everything a red rose means to me. I only hope I get the chance to tell you in person. There are 2 tickets in your name at Will-Call for the game tonight. Tickets will always be waiting for you at each game we play this season. I hope I will see you at one soon. Your dragon man needs you.*

*Boris*

I've put off opening the Sin City Graphix box for as long as I could. But that became kind of impossible to avoid when Parker brings it over and shoves it at me. "Open it, Tallie."

My hands are shaking as I remove the lid. Inside is a denim jacket. But it isn't just any old jacket. It's a stunning, customized work of art with embroidery in Crush colors and embellishments, and DRĂGHICI #90 splayed across the back. ICE DRAGON runs down one sleeve and his dragon is embroidered down the other. It's so pretty I have to sit on the chaise to take it all in, so I don't crumble to the floor in a heap. It's when I remove the tissue from the inside of the jacket and see the label, that I nearly lose it. *KRASOTKA* is embroidered on the collar.

Once I can find my voice, and after swallowing several times to hold back the tears, I tell Parker I've changed my mind.

"I want to go to the game tonight. My puck-money dragon man needs me there."

I TAKE AN EXTRA-LONG SHOWER—SO long that Parker bangs on the door to tell me to hurry my "cute ass" up. She French braids my hair into two long braids and puts me in the same leather leggings I wore before and a cute white top unworn with the tags still on, so it hasn't had the opportunity to be slopped with mustard or ketchup yet, but give me an hour or two and I'll probably get 'er there. I'm being realistic because you know, white shirts and me? Not a good track record. I'll keep buying them though because I'm a baller like that. I layer my fancy Boris jacket over the white top and slip into some strappy red heels I really hope I can walk in, but damn, they do look pretty on my feet.

Parker proclaims me "Ice Dragon approved" before shooing me out of the apartment.

We walk to the arena; the noise getting louder as we approach. There is a band playing. Like, a marching band. There are women dressed in show-girl costumes with huge feather-plumed headpieces and teeny-tiny bikini tops. There are magicians and fire-breathers. It's like a circus, a crazy menagerie of entertainers that totally sum up what Las Vegas is all about.

Fans mill about, some drinking beer out of plastic Crush cups. They take pictures with the entertainers. Parker loves the whole crazy thing, but I'm fixated on the larger-than-life posters of Crush players, displayed brazenly all the way around the arena. When I see Boris's poster, my stomach flips.

Parker elbows me to get my attention but follows my gaze. "Ah. I see what's got your attention. He is such a hottie."

"He's pretty hot," I agree. "But he's more than that, too."

"Why do you torture yourself like this?"

"Like what?"

"Like, tossing him to the curb and then staring longingly at his photo as if you've lost your best friend?"

"I haven't lost my best friend. I have you."

"You know what I mean, Tallie. You're clearly head over heels for this guy."

"He said he thinks he loves me."

"Right after he rescued you from a bunch of underworld dudes. You'd been through a whole ordeal. He probably felt really emotional."

I give a whole-body sigh, gazing longingly back up at Boris's poster. "Boris is a one-woman guy. Like, he wants to fall in love once and that's it. And I worry that...I worry I can't be that for him. His forever girl. You know? I'm not—he's just really good and perfect, you know? He deserves someone perfect, too."

"And you're not?"

"No."

"And you think he is?"

"I mean, no one is *perfect*—"

"Exactly. You're making shit up so you can justify that you're scared about what you're feeling. You found your guy. *The* guy. And he believes you're *the* girl. So why don't you just admit it, get together, and get on with your lives together?"

I bite my lip, thinking.

Parker adds, "Unless something about the kidnapping is holding you back?"

I look at her sharply. "It wasn't his fault."

"I didn't say it was."

I grit my teeth. "I guess I-I know he's too trusting of people. Maybe not as much now that I've pointed out how much money they stole from him, but he acted naïvely—for years—and I guess—I guess I feel that maybe I got hurt because of that naïveté."

*And there it is. The thought I haven't voiced. To anyone.*

Parker pulls me into her arms for another long hug. She says, "That's a very valid thought and I'll bet he thinks it even more than you do. I think you need to go talk to someone about your PTSD. But I also think you need to forgive Boris. I think you need to forgive him and let him love you the way you deserve to be loved. He seems like a great guy with a huge heart. We should all be so lucky."

I know she's right. He's tried to apologize a million times. He feels guilty about what happened, that he totally blames himself. But really, how could he have known who these guys were? They took advantage of him in every possible way. I have to let this go. I have to get past it.

Perhaps the hardest thing about being fast-tracked through school and college was always feeling out of my depth. So young. Excluded. Emotionally behind. I never learned to read social cues well, because all the girls in particular, were far more worldly and never helped me get past that. Part of the leftover fear has inhibited me in forming relationships.

Ultimately, though, I didn't read Boris wrong. He never played with me or my feelings, or misled me. I know that now. But a week ago, I was locked in my darkness, fearing what other things could go wrong in my life. *So, before that could happen, I pushed one of the few very good things in my life away.* But if he has forgiven my behavior, I can see that it's time for me to do the same. After all, he too was thrust into an adult world much younger than he was ready for. Largely, he rose above that and became a man of compassion, empathy, and honor. And I am completely and utterly in love with him.

I turn back and snap a picture of the huge poster and then text it to Boris,

> Talia: I'm here with Parker and can't wait for the Quidditch match to begin.

Talia: Hope you catch the golden snitch.

Boris: ??

Talia: It's a Harry Potter reference.

Boris: I do not know Harry Potter.

Talia: There is no possible way you have never heard of Harry Potter. Have you lived under a rock?

Boris: Still no.

Talia: This isn't happening. There's no way I can be in love with someone who doesn't know about Harry Potter.

Boris: Are you saying you're in love with me?

Talia: If I was???

Boris: I would be a very happy man.

Talia: Well, be happy then. And go light the lamp for me, because I'll be in the stands cheering for my dragon man tonight.

PARKER and I have the best seats, right behind the Crush penalty box. There's a huge pre-game show and the arena feels electric as a video plays, showing highlights from the preseason games. The music is loud, so loud that the bass rattles in my chest. Parker and I drink beer and eat pizza and dance, and when they finally announce the team, we go crazy, screaming and cheering, particularly for a certain star forward.

The team skates around the ice and I can tell Boris is looking for me. I get worried that maybe he won't recognize me with my hair in braids, but then realize my black glasses probably mark me, no matter what I wear. He sees me on the second pass, a grin breaking out on his amazingly handsome face. Butterflies are all up in my stomach at the sight of him. I blow him a kiss and he smiles even wider.

"Goddamn," Parker says, fanning herself. "That was some crazy chemistry I just witnessed."

"He's—" I don't even finish the thought, instead shaking my head and blowing a big breath out by puffing my cheeks.

"Yep," Parker says. She gets me.

BORIS JUST SCORED his second goal of the night. He's a machine. The team is a machine. The words ICE DRAGON are up on the jumbotron, with a crazy graphic of a dragon with a face that looks oddly like a mix of him and the tattoo that snakes up his arm.

"That's my man," I yell. Parker and I are arm in

arm, jumping up and down like we just met the Beatles or something.

"That's your man," she yells.

The game has been fast and furious, with the opposing team out for blood. They want to prove that the Crush are all hype, but the Crush have played with pride, allowing only one goal to their three. Big Viktor Demoskev is a wall of defensive strength. Parker swoons over him, but I elbow her and inform her, "He's engaged to Scarlett...who happens to be six months pregnant." I make a pregnant belly gesture with my hands. "She's sweet. I met her in the First Wives Club at the other game."

"Boo, all the good ones are taken," she says, pouting.

"There's a single guy for ya." I point out Tyler and tell her he will definitely flirt with her if she wants him to. "He thinks flirting with random women is his superpower."

"I won't complain if he comes along with us after the game, he's hot!" Later when he gets the final goal for the Crush, deflected off his stick to go five-hole (between the goalie's legs) from a slap shot by Boris no less, she is jumping up and down like a lunatic cheering for him. The jumbotron shows a replay of his goal and LOCKHARDT LOCKS IT DOWN blasted across the screen over his celly (celebration after scoring) while the thundering crowd nearly brings the walls down it's so insanely loud.

The post-game celebration is just as wild. The noise is ridiculous, my ears ringing from all the screaming. I text Boris to remind him about Parker being here with me and if he could ask Tyler to come by and meet her after they are finished. He tells me it's a done deal already and to wait for them outside the south entrance.

About a half hour later, he comes out showered and looking damn fine in his blue pinstripe Euro-cut suit paired with brown loafers. His still damp hair is slightly mussed, upping his hotness quotient again— if that's even possible. Teammate Tyler looks just as fancy in his window-pane gray suit and purple shirt. Hockey players are quite the clothes horses, but I'm just here to watch and learn.

"Boris, I'd like to formally introduce you to my best friend in all the world, Parker Reaves. Parker, meet Boris, also known as the Ice Dragon."

They shake hands and then Boris introduces Tyler to Parker, who promptly gives her a kiss to the cheek before turning to me. "Hot librarian, it's good to see you again."

"You as well," I say as Boris reaches out to take my hand in his. He tells Tyler and Parker to lead the way, as we start to walk in the vague direction of the Strip. I have no idea where we're going and really, I don't care because I just need to spend some time with Boris. It feels like a month since I've seen him, but it's only been one week. A painfully horrible, long, torturous week though.

We fall back a bit from Parker and Tyler who seem to have hit it off as they chat away like they've known each other for ages.

"You wore the jacket." He looks down at me and squeezes my hand. "You came to be my good luck charm when I needed you. It means a lot."

"I'm so sorry, Boris, for pushing you away. It wasn't right for me to do it that way. Forgive me—"

"No, I should be sorry. I feel sick about how fast I rushed things with you and pushed you. And the way I behaved at your office, I wasn't myself that day."

"Well, the office sex wasn't so bad." I'm grinning. "Honestly, I just didn't know where to put all the feelings, you know? There was so much intensity and I just...I hadn't really dealt with the thing that happened, and then you were saying the L word, and then there's the part about you being so honorable and so good that I wasn't sure I was good enough for you."

He looks utterly shocked. "You didn't think you were good enough for me? Talia, I am just a hockey player. You are a highly educated, highly successful, genius financial planner. You are smart and sexy and bold and exciting. I'm a really, really boring dude, and I can barely read. If anyone's not good enough in this relationship, it's me."

A weird laugh pops out of me. "Umm, no. Just say *no* to that noise, Boris. You are in no way boring. Not to me or to anyone for that matter. Have you seen the ginormous poster of your hot self on the side of the arena? Sweet Christ, every woman in Vegas probably wants you."

"They want the idea of me," he says. "They want to have sex with a pro athlete. They never cared to get to know me, so those sorts of women have never held my interest. You? You interest me. You have a bright mind. You have things to say. You have respect for yourself."

"Well, they can't have you anyway, because you're mine." I stop and turn slightly to show him the back of the jacket. "I've got your name on my back to prove—"

He shuts me up with a blistering kiss and then takes his time kissing me more slowly until I'm breathless and more than a little wobbly on my strappy red heels.

When wolf whistles ring out around us, we start walking again, hand in hand a few more blocks until Tyler leads us into a smallish bar with a live band. There are lots of people in Crush gear and they all want selfies and autographs with Tyler and Boris. Tyler seems to love the attention, while Boris seems to simply tolerate it. Eventually though, we're able to sit down in a booth.

"I have one serious question," Boris says to the group once we've each got a beer. "Who the hell is Harry Potter?"

We all burst out laughing. Parker says, "The boy who lived?"

Boris looks woefully confused.

Tyler says, "Dude, it's a book series about a bunch of kid wizards. It's an international phenomenon."

"A book series..." Boris sinfully strokes his beard scruff. "Okay. It makes sense that I've not heard of it, then."

"Read a book, brother," Tyler says, rolling his eyes. To Parker, he asks, "Wanna go do a shot at the bar?"

Parker smiles and nods, happily hopping up to escape yet another of my long-winded treatises on the everlasting value of Harry Potter and the injustice that the series will probably never be considered a literary classic, even though it totally should be.

I do force this on my sweet Boris though, who listens attentively enough, but seems visibly relieved when I finally stop babbling so he can kiss me again. He's not let go of my hand since we sat down in the booth. He smells as delicious as he looks, and my heart is light for the first time in weeks. Boris has me tucked up against his side like he'll never let me go again when he whispers, "You are beautiful tonight, *krasotka*. I very much like your hair in these braids." He gives one a light tug and his eyes darken with a hunger that I've seen a time or two before. The electric jolt that hits me right between my legs requires me to squirm a little in my seat.

"You are pretty beautiful yourself, dragon man."

We count as Parker and Tyler each do three shots in succession. I have a feeling my best friend is going to play the role of puck bunny tonight and indeed, an hour later, she and Tyler announce they are going back to his place to make waffle fries in his new deep fryer. I think it might be code for having sex but then again, maybe they just have the munchies.

Boris and I head out, too, back to our building. We go to my apartment so I can check on LuLu, who makes a big fuss over her favorite guy—clearly missing him for being absent in her life lately. I can't help watching the two of them as he makes it up to her, speaking Russian to her in the sweetest voice. Gah, this man. He slays me dead with his swoony ways.

After making sure she's fed, I step over to the bookshelf and point to the row of hardcover special edition Harry Potters—among the most prized out of all my books.

"Wow, there are seven of these books?"

I nod. "Yep, and they get more and more complex as they go on. It's a great story. I've read the series three times all the way through." There's way more pride in my voice than is warranted over this particular achievement, I suppose. It makes me blush.

Boris comes to my side and runs a fingertip over my now most certainly pink cheek. "You're very cute when you go full nerd. Maybe you can read these stories to me?"

"Maybe we can start by watching the movies," I suggest.

"Fine, but I have a special place in my heart for listening to you read, as you know." His tone is darker as his eyes flash with mischief.

"I don't think that place is in your heart exactly," I joke.

He takes both of my hands in his. "Talia, I'm so sorry I rushed things. It's just that I am a one-woman man. I do not want something cheap or meaningless and I am pretty sure what I feel for you is real. It's just that the way I was raised has framed my feelings for how I want my life to be as an adult. My upbringing wasn't great. I've not told you why I'm the way I am about relationships, but there is a reason for it, I suppose."

"Will you tell me? I want to know about you too, Boris. The good and the bad." I tug him by the hand over to sit beside me on the chaise, snuggling into his side when he puts his arm around me.

He takes a big breath before he begins to speak. "My bio states my parents divorced when I was young, but the truth is they were never married. My father already had a wife and a family in Romania when he made my mother pregnant with me. After my birth, she took me to live in Prague, because she had friends from college who lived and worked there. She struggled as a single mother but made a decent home for us. My father provided support for me growing up, but she never got over his rejection of us. She did not have a good opinion of herself and took up with all kinds of men who used her and tossed her away like she was nothing. She developed a severe drinking problem and her health deteriorated after that. I was nearly removed from her care by the children's services authorities when she was at her worst. It was Georg's father, her cousin, who reached out and invited her to come back home to Saint Petersburg when she was in dire need of help and support from her family. He is the one who helped me get a spot in the Olympic hockey program with Georg. He was my coach."

My heart nearly breaks from his sad, sad story, and

it takes every ounce of determination not to start weeping for innocent Boris being scared and afraid for his mom and nowhere to turn. I put my hand over his heart and rub softly. "I'm so sorry you had to endure such a scary situation as a young boy all alone, it must have been terrifying for you at home, and then struggling in school. Oh, I'm so sorry, Boris, but it does sound like you got some help and support from Georg's family, so I'm very grateful for them." He covers my hand with his, pressed over his heart, holding it there. "Is your mother still in Saint Petersburg?"

"Yes. She lives in an assisted living facility. I make sure she has everything she needs. Her health is not very good so she needs the care, but she is sober now and is living the best life that she can, I think. She watches my games on the NHL app I set up for her, so she can follow me. I get texts from her after nearly every game once she is able to watch it due to the time difference." He looks at me and runs a finger down my cheek. "She knows about you. About how I feel about you."

"Well, I can certainly understand why you weren't interested in a swinging lifestyle once you grew up. I get it loud and clear now, but I wish you'd told me this before."

"I know, I should have told you that in my future I see a stable home, a loving relationship, and the healthy family life I never had. I want that. I deserve that. But mostly, I want to have it with you, even though I know you aren't ready to hear it from me."

"Oh, I think I might be ready now," I say softly. "And of course, you deserve it," I tell him fervently, my hand on his cheek. "Boris, I knew what I was feeling for you was the real thing, but right after my ordeal, it was...it was a whole lot, all at once. I was wrong to shut you out. I should have been an adult and talked to you about it."

"Was it...were you struggling after the—"

"I was. I am. I think I didn't know how to process what had happened. What I was feeling. But I will seek out therapy for my PTSD, and I promise not to let it come between us."

"When I got that text, Talia, I would rip through worlds to get to you, to protect you."

"I'm not always the one who needs protecting, Boris, as you need protecting too. You're far too trusting. You need someone looking out for you."

"Well, I hope that person will be you. You are fierce and scary."

I laugh and wiggle off the chaise and over to the shelves. "Yes, I'll always be there to hit someone over the head with a book." I pull the first Harry Potter from the shelf and say, "I'll read two chapters, okay?"

He grins and pulls me to the chaise, settling his head on my lap. I read the first two chapters, and then Boris surprises me when he pulls the book from my hands and rearranges our positions, my head on his lap. After reading a full page out loud to me in his sexy accent that I love to hear, he tells me about the work he's been doing to better manage his dyslexia.

Honestly, seeing him reading turns me on.

The tables have turned.

I close the book and set it safely on the side table, before straddling myself over his lap.

"You are so amazing, and I am very turned on right now. I likey when you read to me." I press my mouth to his. He answers in kind, pushing hard, his tongue insistent against my lips. I moan as I give him access, his hands against my back, his cock hardening beneath my hips, hitting between my legs at just the right spot. I move my hips, the frustration of being fully clothed making me growl like a wild animal in mating season.

I roll off him and start peeling off my clothes. "I want to be naked with you. And I want...I want—" I'm scared to say it.

"You want what, *krasotka*? Tell me." He doesn't say it sweetly, rather it's a hard command demanding a response.

"I want—you to f-fuck me this time. I want us to... fuck it out. We both need that very much right now, I think."

He chuckles darkly as he undresses, nodding slowly up and down, affirming he indeed does agree. I get a full view of his perfectly sculpted body when he stands naked and ready for me. Flawless pectorals, washboard abs, wide shoulders, trim waist. His legs are strong and muscular. His big cock juts toward me, rock hard and ready as he stares hungrily when I drop my bra to the floor.

I'm now as naked as him.

*I'm such a lucky, lucky girl.*

"Lie back on the chaise," he commands.

I sink down into the blue velvet and try to control my racing heartbeat from leaping out of my chest.

"Rub your nipples and let me watch you get your sweet pink pussy ready to take my hard cock."

Pinching and twisting my nipples with one hand, I finger my clit with the other until I'm so slippery and wet for him I can hardly stand it. I might come just thinking about having him inside me with the way he's being so gruff and hard and sexy and dominant.

"I want to fuck your pretty mouth and hold you by your braids."

*Oh. My. God.*

Boris's eyes are hooded and dark as he moves to hover over me, his cock kissing my lips before I open my mouth to take him in. I have to stretch wide to take him, but I do, and I let him push deep to the back of my throat. He does what he said he wanted to do with my braids, wrapping one around each fist, and using them to fuck his cock in and out of my mouth. It's dirty and filthy and glorious and wonderful. He fucks like he does everything else. Carefully and with attention to detail. I take him as deep as I can until I can taste the salt of precum and he releases me. He pulls me by the legs to the edge of the chaise and spreads me wide open. His cock at my entrance, he sinks it fiercely into me, deep and hot and hard.

I asked for hard. He gives it hard. In and out. Harder and faster. His biceps bulge from holding himself above me as he pushes his cock as deep as he can go. I love it. I'm delirious with pleasure. I climax in rapid succession and feel tears on my face. I'm out of my body and no longer know where Boris ends, and Talia begins. There's no separation of us, just we.

With a roar Boris shudders into me, his cock twitching and jerking the last of his climax out of him and into me. He collapses on top of me, both of us struggling to catch our breath.

We lie on my blue velvet chaise for a long time, kissing and caressing each other with softer touches of lips and hands than a few moments ago.

Time slows down.

Nothing is more important than this right now.

Finally, he speaks. "I can't stand it. I need to say it, *krasotka*."

I bite back a smile. "I know you do. And I love you, too."

# epilogue

Boris

*Four months later.*

The team is heading into winter break and I am very much ready for the time off. It has been an amazing season, made better by seeing Talia in the stands at nearly every game—even the ones on the road. She really is my good luck charm. I convinced her by pleading my case that if her being at the games helps me to score more goals so the Crush can win more than they lose, well then you keep doing it. Hockey players are superstitious as fuck, and I'm not ashamed admitting it.

Talia is feeling better too, after finding a therapist to help her through her PTSD from the abduction. Having someone to listen and tell you it wasn't your fault is powerful medicine toward healing the mind of painful burdens. My investors in Russia went silent in the aftermath; and I have never heard from them again. The gun fight was all over the local news immediately after it happened, speculated as a drug deal gone wrong. Two were dead at the scene and the third died at the hospital a day or two later, so there was never a witness to make a statement. Heisenberg's guys were ghosts in the whole thing, so no connection there either. The reports dwindled away as soon as the next crime story took center stage in the local news, and people quickly forgot about the mysterious Vegas underworld shooting resulting in three dead criminals with fake visas. Those three got exactly what they deserved in my opinion. Karma, you know. I don't lose sleep over it anymore.

It helps that my investments are doing much better, my wealth starting to take real shape under Talia's close attention. I can fly her first class to any road games she wants to attend, upgrade our hotel rooms, and take her out to amazing places with me. It's fun, traveling with her, exploring the cities we visit, growing closer as the months pass. For Los Angeles and Anaheim games we always make time for a visit to the home where she grew up with her parents and three siblings—two older brothers and a younger sister. They have welcomed me with open arms, though it has taken a bit getting used to so many smart, nerdy people in one family. Her father is a university professor of astronomy, her mother is the principal of a high school, her brother Deryk, the CEO of a computer engineering firm he founded, her brother Alec, a lawyer, and her little sister, Dahlia, at just eighteen, has already completed two years at university, studying to become a veterinarian. So many super-intelligent humans under one roof can be overwhelming, but the dinner conversation is never boring. I am *always* learning something new from listening to them go full-nerd on every topic imaginable over plates of her mom's lasagna or her dad's grilled tri-tip.

When we arrive at the airport, Talia puts her hand on my arm and asks, "Are you sure you want to travel though? We're on the go all the time for games. I thought maybe you'd want a break from airplanes and buses and hotel rooms?"

"I'm good with this travel, *krasotka*."

"When are you going to tell me where we're going?"

"You'll find out in another minute I think."

We check in at the first-class counter and I hand over my identification. "To Orlando," the attendant says.

"Yes," I confirm.

When I glance over at Talia, she gives me a funny look. I can see her trying to puzzle it out. "What's in Orlando?"

"The Wizarding World of Harry Potter." I'm unable to contain my grin for a second longer.

Her eyes go wide, and she jumps up and down, clapping her hands in delight. "Harry Potter World? Really?"

"Really, *krasotka*." She hurls herself into my arms and kisses me until her glasses fall off her beautiful face. I set her on her feet, put her glasses back into place, and then press my forehead to hers. "I am thrilled you approve of my choice."

"Thrilled is an understatement, my love, and you always choose perfectly because you've got game."

"You think that I've got game? Me?" She can't be serious.

"So much game, dragon man, so, so much."

"I think you're just saying that because you love me, *krasotka,* and you really want to go to Harry Potter World."

She shakes her head no. "I love you of course, but it's irrelevant to your level of game-ness at any given time. Have you forgotten all those precious love notes you sent to woo me back to you, along with enough roses to fill a barn? Your love notes beat out Harry Potter World by a mile on a scale of woo-worthiness. Seriously."

"Oh, I remember writing the notes, *krasotka.* I dictated it first into my phone and then I enlarged the font size and copied it onto paper. It took a long time, though I did get faster the more I practiced."

"I rest my case. Not just another pretty face, folks, but whip-smart too. How did I get so lucky?"

As my *krasotka* chatters away, we head toward security and our boarding gate. She likes talking about so many things all the time, and I can honestly say it makes me happy to listen to her. But I still have fun teasing her whenever I get an opportunity. "I don't know. You won the boyfriend lottery maybe?" I suggest.

"That and don't forget your wooing skills," she

reminds me. "You could teach the class on wooing and hand out certificates to the guys who passed it. I'm thinking, Tyler for example, could certainly benefit from your vast and intricate knowledge on the topic of how to properly woo someone."

"So, are you trying to say I am good at the wooing?"

I can barely keep a straight face when she goes quiet, because that's when I know she's onto me messing with her.

"Don't push your luck, dragon man. I know what you did there." She gives my hand a squeeze for emphasis.

I take her hand to my lips and kiss the top of it. "You can take it out on me when we get there."

"Oh, you can bet on it." Her eyes spark with a certain look that makes me hard.

*I can't fucking wait.*

AN HOUR LATER, we're seated in first class about to take off, when Talia puts her head on my shoulder. "I'm so excited. Thank you for this. It's going to be pure magic, you'll see."

I pull a small box from my pocket and hand it to her. "What's this?" she asks.

"You have to open it, *krasotka.*" She takes the tiny box and shakes it next to her ear. When she removes the lid and sees what's inside, she can't help squealing a little. I'm pretty sure she likes it.

The Harry Potter-themed charm bracelet comes out of the box and is slipped onto her wrist. "I love it so much and I love you. Thank you." She admires for it a moment more and then leans over and offers her lips to me for a kiss.

I never pass up an offer to kiss my girl.

"It's a promise I *will* keep, *krasotka*." I point out the silver charm that reads "Always."

"Always, Boris." Within her stormy blue eyes, I can only see the love I have for her and the love she has for me shining radiantly up at me.

"Always, *krasotka* Natalia."

*I do believe it will be.*

# my thoughts about...

# afterword

Extensive creative license was applied in portraying some elements of NHL games, fan events and awards, that would **not happen in real life**. I did this intentionally to create a more enjoyable reading experience within the storyline. These stories have been carefully crafted for your reading pleasure and in no way meant to be a true and accurate representation of NHL best practices and/or official rules currently or in the past.

Hockey Romance F-I-C-T-I-O-N all the way!!!

# vegas crush by trope

All books in the *VEGAS CRUSH* series are *STANDALONES* existing in a connected world centering around a Las Vegas ice-hockey team. You can read them out of order if you wish and everything will still make sense with only minor spoilers. I've made a list of tropes for you here.

## CRUSHED

BOOK 1

Forbidden, Reformed "Player", Ukrainian/American Hero, Good Girl Heroine, Office Romance, Love in the Workplace, He Falls First, Sports Romance, Team Captain, Social Media Manager, Risking it All for Love, Band of Brothers

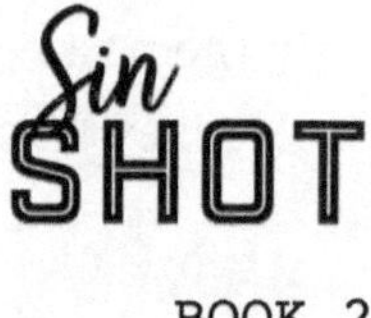


BOOK 2

Bad Boy Russian Hero, Virgin Heroine, Damaged Heroine, Forbidden, Office Romance, Hockey Defenseman, Team Physical Therapist, Love in the Workplace, Band of Brothers, Overcoming Self-Doubt and Addiction, Trust

# ROCKET

BOOK 3

Grumpy/Sunshine, Russian Hero, Feisty Red-Haired Heroine, Forbidden, Office Romance, Hockey Defenseman, Public Relations Manager, Love in the Workplace, He Falls First, Brooding Alpha, Opposites Attract, Band of Brothers

# MONEY

BOOK 4

Opposites Attract, Forbidden Romance, Financial Advisor/Client Relationship, Russian/Romanian Hero, Nerdy Young Heroine, Fresh Start in Vegas, Dyslexic Hero, Gentleman Alpha, Good Guy Hero, He Falls First, Age Gap, Vegas Mafia Suspense, Savior Hero, Band of Brothers, Superstar Hockey Centerman

BOOK 5

Friends to Lovers, Teammates Little Sister, Young Virgin Heroine, Russian Heroine, Boston Native, Bad Boy Hero, Forbidden Romance, First Love, Age Gap, Single "Dad" Vibes, Hardscrabble Upbringing, Band of Brothers, Hockey Defenseman, New Adulting, Found Family

BOOK 6

Enemies to Lovers, Forced Proximity, Love in the Workplace, Neuro-Diverse Hero, French-Canadian Hero, Rock Chick Heroine, Socially Awkward w/ No Filter, Opposites Attract, Instant Attraction, Fish Out of Water, Band of Brothers, Superstar Hockey Goalie, Rockstar Heroine, Brooding Alpha, Guitar Lessons w/ Cute Kids, Personal Growth, Sacrificing for Love

BOOK 7

Surprise Pregnancy, One Night Stand, Forbidden Romance, Love in the Workplace, Boss/Employee, Office Romance, Sneaky Dates, Instant Attraction, Age Gap, Mature Hero, Gentleman Alpha, Love After Divorce, Can't Keep Their Hands off Each Other, Career Milestones, Team General Manager, Team Nutritionist

BOOK 8

Friends With Benefits, Instant Attraction, He Falls First, Brooding Alpha, Superhero Complex, Gentleman Alpha, Damsel in Distress, Knight in Shining Armor, Living up to Father's Legacy, Vegas Mafia Suspense, Comic Book Nerd, Wedding Planner Heroine, Band of Brothers, Finding Your Voice, Parent/Child Relationships

BOOK 9

Age Gap, Secret Crush, Surprise Pregnancy, Shotgun Wedding, Opposites Attract, The Owner's Granddaughter, The Brooding Hockey Player, Forced Proximity, Only 1 Bed, Career Milestones, Forbidden, Old Family Friends, *Neanderthal* Hero, *Heiress* Heroine, Parenthood, Beliefs, Growing Up, Manning Up, Facing Your Demons, Family Legacy

BOOK 10

Christmas Marriage Proposal, No Third-Act Breakup, Proposal Problems, Brooding Hockey Player Hero, Buying a Home, Festive Holidays, Dear Santa Letter, Gentleman Alpha, Building a Legacy, Comic Book Nerd, Wedding Planner Heroine, Team Captain, Band of Brothers, Family Relationships, OTT Romantic Gifts

# about the author

**BRIT DEMILLE** is the alter ego of *NYT* Bestselling author, Raine Miller, having an absolute blast writing books quite different from what she writes as Raine.

Stories about sexy billionaires [millionaires make the cut too] who fall in instalove with young women who may or may not be virgins, and then go on to make adorable babies together are her favorite themes. In addition to the billionaires, hot hockey players are at the top of her list of favorite heroes, along with royals and ex-military bodyguards.

Most important when she writes a story is a happily ever after. But during the actual *writing* of the story, the most important thing is a cup of hot tea with a splash of milk (and don't forget the stash of cherry Jolly Ranchers). A dog or two will likely be in between her and the chair at any given moment, which is very handy, because they are the ones who approve everything she writes.

**RAINE MILLER** is a #2 *New York Times, USA Today,* and *Wall Street Journal* bestselling author since 2012. Before that, she spent two decades teaching kiddos to read—something she's most proud of. These days, writing steamy romance books pretty much fills up the hours...for which she keeps pinching herself to make absolutely sure she's not dreaming.

#Truth

She has a handsome husband, two amazing sons, and two very bouncy Italian greyhounds to keep her busy the rest of the time. Her boys know she writes romance books but gratefully they have zero interest in reading even a single one. *Thank. God.*

When she's not writing she's likely deep into a hockey game cheering on her beloved *VEGAS GOLDEN KNIGHTS* and dreaming up a new book. The greyhounds are likely to be in her lap while she writes the books or watches hockey—both dogs at the same time of course!

She loves to hear from readers and chat about the characters she's created.

You can connect with Raine on Facebook in her reader group, **Raine Miller Romance Readers.** She pops in to visit most days because it's a super happy place where romance awesomeness abounds day in and day out with the most amazing readers on earth.

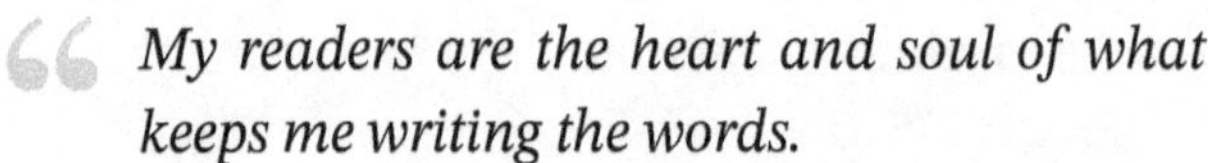

*My readers are the heart and soul of what keeps me writing the words.*

#Truth2

# also by raine miller

**The BLACKSTONE AFFAIR**

NAKED, Part 1

ALL IN, Part 2

EYES WIDE OPEN, Part 3

RARE and PRECIOUS THINGS, Part 4

**The ROTHVALE LEGACY**

PRICELESS, I

MY LORD, II

**BLACKSTONE DYNASTY**

FILTHY RICH, I

FILTHY LIES, II

**HOCKEY ROMANCE *as Brit DeMille***

CRUSHED, Vegas Crush #1

SIN SHOT, Vegas Crush #2

RED ROCKET, Vegas Crush #3

PUCK MONEY, Vegas Crush #4

SMOKESHOW, Vegas Crush #5

The KEEPER, Vegas Crush #6

LUCKY PUCK, Vegas Crush #7

Mr. HOCKEY, Vegas Crush #8

CLUSTERPUCK, Vegas Crush #9

Mr. HOCKEY's MARRY CHRISTMAS, Vegas Crush #10

**CONTEMPORARY ROMANCE**

CHERRY GIRL

HUSBAND MATERIAL

LOVELY PINK

**HISTORICAL ROMANCE**

The MUSE

The PASSION of DARIUS

The UNDOING of a LIBERTINE

*Wedding Night Diaries*

LORD BLACKWOOD'S VIRGIN

# join raine mail

FOR MY NEWSLETTER and information on upcoming books and events, you should definitely sign up for Raine Mail. Use the QR code below.

*whispers* *There's so many freebies in that thing.*

subscribe to Raine Mail